D0233721

2

Hamlet: The People of the Horse

COVENTRY LIBRARIES

Please return this book on or before
the last date stamped below.

PS130553 DISK 4

Coventry City Council

To renew any items:

- visit any Coventry Library
- go online to www.coventry.gov.uk/libraries
- telephone 024 7683 1999

To Steph – for enduring my crazy explorations of Wessex and other magical circles - even in the rain

To Sam – for knocking off a few rough edges and making Archer a little less of a machine

Front cover picture courtesy of English Heritage
     www.english-heritage.org.uk/daysout/properties/kenilworth-castle/
Back cover picture Copyright © 2010 Cheryl St. Germaine
     www.myspace.com/mysts_of_avalon
White Horse design Copyright © 2010 Anthony Askew
     www.ant-askew.co.uk/

First published in 2010 by Lulu

ISBN: 978-1-4461-5021-4

www.lulu.com

www.hengistarcher.co.uk

Prologue

Archer was sixteen when he met Rory for the first time. Actually, that wasn't strictly true. When he was five, Rory's mother Lynette stayed with his first foster parents for a while. At seventeen Lynette was more like a woman, especially because she was going to have a baby. She didn't stay long because of problems with the pregnancy, living somewhere else until the baby arrived.

He saw Lynette several times after that, it was hard to miss her melodic laugh or the smile that brightened up dark corners. She was probably the first female he ever loved and he nursed a passion for her that lasted until he began to take an interest in girls of his own age. Or, more accurately, until they began to take an interest in him. So in fact, he had met Rory before, when he was six and Rory looked exactly like any other baby, tiny and red-faced with a lot of noise at one end and bad smells at the other.

Archer remembered the second time well; he had come in from school, dumped his bags on the desk next to the computer and gone into the kitchen to see what he could scavenge. Penny always had something ready; she knew how hungry a full day at school made them. Some days they were just allowed to help themselves to as much as they wanted from the fruit bowl. Occasionally there were chocolate biscuits with animal names like Penguin, Kit-Kat or Fox. They were only allowed one and woe betide anyone who tried to take more.

The best was when she baked. Not the sweet, artificial tasting muck they called cakes, full of chemicals supposed to make them last longer on shelves somewhere. No, this was freshly baked from wholesome ingredients like honey, oats, real lemons and fruits she had dried herself. Today was one of those days; huge cookies, almost as big as saucers, with apricots and pecan nuts. He crept up to squeeze her waist as usual. She would jump and scold him, but he knew she enjoyed it by the smile on her face. Today there was no smile as she peered down the garden.

'Looking for someone?'

'Yes. It shouldn't take that long to walk back from the den, Tom came back a few minutes ago.'

'Yeah, he was in such a hurry he knocked me over. He muttered something about going to the shop to buy snakes. But there is no pet shop close by, I must have misheard.'

'Could you do me a favour? Walk up the garden and check Rory's alright. I'm probably just fussing but Tom's friends can be a bit rough with the younger ones.'

'Sure no problem. Consider it done.' He took another bite of the cookie, getting a burst of sweet apricot as he passed by the empty greenhouse. There was no-one hiding in the space between the greenhouse and the shed where Tom normally leapt out shouting 'boo'. This was followed by a race to the bottom of the garden; Tom had to reach his den before Archer could catch him and nine times out of ten he let the boy win. Putting the last bite of the cookie in his mouth, Archer passed the vegetable patch and checked behind the fruit trees. All that was left was the den and the compost heap; only someone with a strong stomach or a weak nose would hide there. He heard the sound of voices, a bit of a scuffle, then a scream.

One

When you're only sixteen years old, there are all sorts of changes going on in your body. Nasty little chemicals called hormones cause all sorts of problems with things growing where they shouldn't. You're always falling up stairs and knocking things over because nothing is balanced. Girls seem to be all about giggling, crying and kisses. Boys are all about fighting, being too proud to cry and if you're lucky the odd kiss.

Given all of those problems, what you really need is a bit of a support network, a few people on your side. The last thing you need is to be uprooted from everything you know, everyone you could call a friend and the place you have called home for your whole life. You don't need to be in a strange place, a million miles away from everything and everyone you know and love. Somewhere they apparently speak the same language, using the same words, but in very different ways, with very different meanings. *Who would know that calling someone "bad" actually meant they were really good or saying something was "wicked" meant it was incredibly good? That if you liked someone they were "cool", but if you really liked someone, they became "hot".*

Archer was pleased and proud when he was voted the top male student in his graduating class. Less than a week later, he sat miserably on his bed, wishing he had gained the lowest marks instead of the highest. Then he wouldn't get the daily reminder that only babies slept in cots.

'So mister Archer, are you going to show us how to use your bow and arrows then?'

'He thinks he's Robin Hood, a real bad-ass outlaw.'

'He doesn't realise that you're supposed to give that sort of thing up when you leave junior school.'

'No he still thinks he's a baby, calls his bed a cot.'

But that was what they called beds where he came from, babies slept in cradles. As ever, Archer showed no reaction, it was the only way to deal with that kind of bullying, deny them what they wanted until they got bored and picked on someone else.

It wasn't that this was his first experience of taunts and name-calling, he had put up with far worse. For several years, he endured many fights because his foster parents were a lot older than the other kid's parents. At that point he decided he wasn't going to worry any more, the bullies just weren't important enough for him to care about their taunts. So for the next few years, they stopped just saying and started doing. Things that belonged to him would get damaged, destroyed or disappear. He had an idea who was behind it all, but the boy had many supporters and Archer didn't have a single person he could call a friend, so he just put up and shut up. He smiled as yet another one of the strange phrases came into his head, he was picking up their expressions quickly by spending many of his waking hours studying the magical box in the corner of the room downstairs.

The first time he saw it, he had stared in horror as the screen showed pictures of a battle with great explosions and wounded people.

'Can we not help those people? They need…' but as he was trying to decide how best to treat a leg that was torn off at the knee and pumping blood, the image changed to show a beach with several women wearing almost no clothing. He stared in disbelief as the foster father, a gruff man called Dave, said,

'Close your mouth son, never seen a woman in a bikini before?'

'But how can those women be inside the box? And what happened to the wounded man?'

'Are you for real? Those people are in Spain and the war was somewhere in the Middle East. Didn't they have a telly where you came from?'

'A telly? Is that what you call the box?'

'Yes. They make a programme and send it through the air. The TV gets the signal and displays it on that screen.'

'How do they send programmes through the air?'

'Oh I don't know, radio waves or something. I'm no electrician. I'm sure it'll tell you on the internet. Well it would if Peter hadn't kicked his football into the monitor and smashed it. I suppose you could try the Encyclopaedia Brittanica, it's on the shelf. You can read can't you?'

Archer had barely understood anything the man had said for the last few minutes and he turned to look, feeling great relief as he saw something he could understand. Books. Choosing the one marked S-U, he took it up to his room and lay on the bed, catching up on several hundred years of inventions.

Two

So it became a daily battle with his poor overtired brain to cram as much information in as he could. Not an easy task when he was using so much of his energy to fight off the other inhabitants of the house who were determined to break his spirit. Peter, the son of the house, would be a nice lad if he had been raised on his own or maybe with a sister to soften the rough edges. Instead, the company of two rogues, spoiled by many years of harsh trials and unable to find any kind of inner peace, had spoilt him. If anything, he was worse than Jack and Kyle, as though he had to prove that he was every bit as "hard" as them. He always had to find some way of taking each new scheme to the next level of destruction or torment.

Just by being there, Archer was their natural target. So every waking minute was a test of his ability to detect their latest plot and survive or endure it with as little damage to himself or his surroundings as possible. If they got hurt by his resistance or evasion of their intended punishment he felt no qualm, it was no more than they deserved. However, the over-developed sense of honour instilled into him from many hours of military training meant that he would pull his punches at the last instant so they never felt the full force of his blows.

This reminded him of his friend Finn's campaign to disguise his full strength and convince everyone that Archer was the better contender. He did such a good job that Archer even considered throwing a round to let Finn triumph on his best event. The memory brought an involuntary grin, but Jack noticed it.

'Look guys, he's smiling. He obviously likes this.'

'He's some kind of freak. They've got a name for people who like pain.' Peter had to go one better.

'Satanist or something.' Kyle tried to join in, but he shrivelled at the scorn in Jack's voice as he corrected him.

'No you're thinking of a sadist, that's someone who likes hurting other people.'

'That would be you three then. Sadists.' Archer regretted the provocation as Peter slapped his face. He could not resist as he was strapped to a tree with some kind of contraption they had "borrowed" from Dave's garage. Peter called it a bungee, much too friendly a name for the metal ring with six red limbs, each ending with a potentially lethal hook. Archer's imagination taunted him with images of how the device could be used to inflict all kinds of damage on his body. He quickly threw those thoughts into a compartment in his mind and locked it away before they could spot the alarm on his face.

They had merely used it to restrain him, but his memory insisted on comparing it to a trial from two years earlier. With the help of his gang, Edlyn had tied Archer to a tree, whipped him with branches then stuffed his mouth with the poisonous leaves of a yew tree. There was little difference in the wit or imagination of the two sets of adversaries and it always took superior numbers and dirty tricks to overwhelm him.

'Yeah we're sadists alright and you're just a pussy.'

'He's a scaredy cat, too girly to fight like a man.'

If only they knew. Memories of previous battles fought for his attention, threatening to curl his lip in contempt at their puny attempts to test his will. So he retreated into the battle room within his mind, presenting them with the cold face while his warrior gifts took over and he considered the options. He was sure they continued to fling insults at him, but he was impervious to their words.

Subtly testing the cords binding his body, he felt a little movement in each one. Unlike the thick twine he knew, it yielded as he forced his weight against it. He sensed that the cords would not become taut enough to break without a lot of effort on his part and they would notice before he could work up enough strength to do the job. They had not been very smart about restraining his hands, relying on the tension of the cords round his forearms to contain them. So he could free them without too much difficulty and …

His escape strategy was never completed as an urgent message screamed in from the portion of his brain he'd left on sentry duty. He tuned back in to his aggressors.

'… you stay here and watch him while I go and get an apple and his bow. Back in a tick.'

'So it's gonna be like Robin Hood meets William Tell.'

Archer could not stop the alarm from showing in his eyes and Kyle saw it. 'Finally he wakes up and takes some notice. We've got you worried now haven't we?'

Archer brought the shutters down immediately and his voice was neutral, almost bored. 'Only because I have become used to seeing the world through two eyes. I'm sure I will adjust to having one.'

'What, are you saying he'll miss and hit you in the eye?' Jack seemed fascinated.

'If I'm very unlucky. Has he used a longbow before?'

'I dunno.'

''Course he has. We all had bows and arrows when we was little.'

Archer smiled, knowing that he probably wouldn't even be able to string the bow, let alone pull the string back with sufficient force to shoot an arrow. 'I should have no problem then. He will shoot the apple straight off my head. No part of my body will be pierced by the barbed tip travelling at the speed of an express train.' He had spent many hours reading about the methods of modern transport and he couldn't begin to imagine travelling at speeds four times faster than a galloping horse.

'No way. It can't go as fast as a train, it's only a bit of wood and string.'

'A train travels at one hundred and twenty five miles every hour. A shaft from a longbow travels at one hundred and twenty four miles every hour. I would say that's close.'

'So you could kill someone with your bow?'

Archer fixed Kyle with a hard stare. Of the three of them, he was the one who might possibly have a redeeming feature. He seemed to have paid more attention than the others to the scant studies they seemed to do in this country. Archer was surprised by how little the boys seemed to know about anything, especially important things like the seasons and plants and animals. 'Haven't you read anything about the success of the English longbow in medieval wars? They struck terror into the heart of every Frenchman.'

'Yeah but that's just old-fashioned nonsense. It's all fairy tales like Robin Hood and King Arthur.' Kyle was quick to dismiss them, but Archer knew that all historical tales were based on facts and actual people.

'Well in two minutes Pete's going to come back with your bow and maybe he'll strike terror into your heart. Then you won't be so smug about all your fancy facts and figures.' Jack looked as though he was anticipating this prospect with great enjoyment.

Despite his earlier bravado, Archer jumped as the back door opened.

Three

It was not Peter but his mother Julie, calling them in for dinner. They both ran off and Archer considered for a second the idea of freeing himself using the strategy he'd worked out. A moment's deliberation told him that he had more to gain by letting them think he was helpless in this constraint. They would be more likely to use it again which would put him at an advantage. Sure enough, a few minutes later Kyle came out and fiddled at the back of the tree then the cords dropped one pair at a time. Grabbing the device, Kyle stuffed it under his jumper, fixing on his fiercest face as he threatened, 'You'd better not say anything, or you'll be in serious trouble.'

Trying to give the impression of someone intimidated by such threats, Archer ran back to the house and straight up to his room. There was no sign of Peter, but every cupboard and drawer had been emptied, the contents strewn on the floor. Dave walked past and looked in. 'I don't know how you lived before, but we keep things tidy in this house. Get that lot cleared before you come down to dinner.'

Closing the door, Archer bent down next to the bed and felt underneath. He'd tied a couple of loops of string on either end of the frame and the bow was nestling in the loops. He'd read about a security device called a yale lock, he would buy one of these with the money Lynette had left him and fit it to the door so no-one could enter his room without his permission. He did not have many possessions so it did not take long to restore order to the room, but one of the books had a page torn and Julie said she would get him some Sellotape after the meal.

It was a minute's job to repair the tear so that it was almost invisible fix, then he watched her use the tape to wrap up a box of what she called chocolates. She offered him one from another box and he took the brightly coloured package and stared at it uncertainly.

'It's hazelnut, don't you like them? There's a strawberry cream or caramel if you can't have nuts.'

He watched as she pulled the two ends apart and it untwisted. Copying her actions, he saw that under the purple crackly material was a shiny silver wrapper covering a lump of something brown and shiny. He hesitated, its appearance was too close to something he knew was not normally eaten by humans. It was shaped and patterned to look like a nut and did not smell offensive. Holding it closer to his nose, he sniffed a milky scent. Tentatively sticking out his tongue, he licked it, fearing the worst and pleasantly surprised by the sweet taste. Biting through a small portion, he felt the explosion of flavour as it melted inside his mouth. He was smitten.

She was watching him curiously. 'Have you never had chocolate before?'

He shook his head, unable to reply as he had just taken a bite containing hazelnut, something he recognised.

'I've heard of people who won't have a telly in the house, but not to give a kid chocolate, that's really mean.'

'They are not mean, we have plenty of sweetmeats, made with honey or fruit. How do you grow chocolate?'

'I'm not sure if we can grow cocoa beans in this country. It's all made in hot places like Brazil. You probably could in a greenhouse. Here, have another one.'

'Thank you. Why does this one only have one jacket when the others have two?'

'Jacket? Oh you mean wrapper. No, they all have one unless there's been an accident on the machine and they get double wrapped.'

'This one just has the shiny wrapper.'

'Foil.'

'You mean like a sword for fencing?' He had read about modern day fencing with foils and epees, it was as close as he would get to the sports he knew.

She looked curious. 'You do seem to know about some strange things. How would you know about a fencing foil but not know about the silver foil we use to wrap food in?'

'My people live simple lives. We don't have much in the way of techonol – technology.'

'Silver foil isn't technology, it's been around forever. Well, since the fifties anyway.'

'The eighteen fifties?'

'I was actually thinking of the nineteen fifties. You know, after the second world war when they were doing all that space-race stuff. I don't know, I wasn't very good at history at school. I was more into English and the arts.'

'So this silver foil is used to wrap food in. Why would you need to wrap chocolate? Surely the chocolate is already wrapped around the nut.'

'Because if it gets hot, the chocolates will melt and stick together.'

'But they are in this paper box.'

'Cardboard. It's like stiff paper.'

'Why do you not just put this cardboard box somewhere cool so they won't melt?'

'It does sound simple when you put it like that, but these were probably made a few months ago and the sell by date is,' she turned the box over and several of the chocolates fell out. 'Oops. Here, it's March next year.'

'I can see they might need something to separate them if they are going to be kept for so many months, but I don't see why you would need this extra wrapper.' Gathering up the sweets, he put them back in the box.

'The cellophane? I don't know. It makes them look pretty and I suppose it helps you to tell the flavours apart. Why don't you have a couple of those?'

'No thank you, they are quite strong.'

'Well you are the strange one. I've never known a kid refuse chocolate before.'

He shrugged. 'I'm sorry to ask so many questions but there is so much here that I don't understand.'

'Don't you worry love, it's a pleasure to have a lad take such an interest. You ask away.'

'I'm still confused by the purpose of this decorated paper. Is paper not a precious thing here?'

She laughed. 'You sound just like my sister Dawn, she's a real eco-warrior. Sorry, that's someone who cares about the environment. She recycles everything; separates out all the glass and cans, paper and plastic, even the foil lids from the butter. And never talk to her about carrier bags, that's like her own personal crusade. She was thrilled when some of the big stores started selling re-usable bags.'

Archer didn't understand half of the words she had used, but the sentiment was clear. 'It sounds very much like my people. Every basin of water we wash in is used again to wash the animals. Water used to clean vegetables is then poured over the growing plants. But paper takes such a lot of time and energy to make that it is only used when something is worth writing down.'

'So how do you learn things at school?'

'We use slates and chalk. Each child has one notebook for writing down important things, but everything else is stored in the mind.'

'Don't you forget things? I could never remember all the formulas in science without writing them down.'

'If you need to use it you will remember it, otherwise there are books in the librarie that everyone can use.'

'That does sound sensible, we get so much junk mail every day and all the free newspapers nobody ever reads.' She sighed. 'You've made me feel guilty now about this wrapping paper, but if I didn't wrap it, she would know what it was and there would be no surprise. Do you not wrap gifts?'

'Oh I see now. We do the same, but we use gift bags made from cloth that can be re-used. The men usually give the plain bag but the women make them pretty with ribbons and flowers and fruit.'

'Sounds like here, men just give gifts in the shop's carrier bag. Most people like to tear the paper off and throw it away, we don't worry about the waste. But Dawn always opens it carefully and uses the paper to wrap another present.'

Archer thought about the conversation later as he researched eco-warrior in the encyclopaedia. It really seemed as though the people in this country had very little respect for the natural world around them. In the short time he had lived here he observed a total lack of respect for the environment and its precious resources. There was so much waste of food, time, energy, effort and materials.

This was so at odds with everything he had been brought up to believe in, he thought there must be something fundamentally different about this place. As he gradually explored the countryside around the small village, he realised that it was similar to the place he lived. There were hills and valleys, fields and rivers and the same types of trees, although a lot fewer of them. He saw very few animals apart from the family pets; usually overfed, under-exercised dogs and cats with no real purpose apart from eating and sleeping. Then one day, he finally connected with somewhere that reminded him of home.

Four

'We're going to visit my sister Dawn this weekend, I hope you'll come with us.' Julie smiled as she asked.

'Are the others going?' Archer was wary.

'Jack and Kyle won't be. They're spending the day round at Brett's house and sleeping the night. We'll be stopping the night with her, it's quite a long drive and Dave likes to have a drink with her husband Phil.'

'Where do they live?' Since discovering the atlas, Archer had developed a thirst for geography. Every time he heard or read about a new place, he would go and look it up, building up his own picture of this strange world.

'Somerset. Cider country. You'll no doubt be drinking some of that, just be careful, the rough stuff can be pretty strong. And before you ask, it's made from apples.' Dave was not as patient with Archer's questions as his wife.

'Is that north of here?'

'No, west of Glastonbury. About ninety miles.'

'But that's a three day journey.'

'If you walked. It's just under three hours in the car.'

Archer shut his mouth, not wanting to appear stupid in front of Peter who walked in looking annoyed. 'Do I 'ave to go to Dawn's? Why can't I go with the others?'

'Because Brett's Mum only has room for two, and anyway it's Geena's birthday.'

'Why would I want to go to a three-year-old's party?'

'Because she's your cousin and Dawn will be expecting you. If you play your cards right Phil might let you and Archer go out on the tractor.'

'That's kid's stuff.'

'You seemed to like it last time.'

'I was a kid last time.'

'It was only two years ago.'

'Yeah, well a lot happens in two years.'

Archer couldn't believe that a son would talk to his mother with so little respect, he had never experienced that before. He knew better than to react to anything that went on involving Peter or the others, it only gave them more reasons to make trouble for him. He wanted to offer Julie some help with the preparations but he knew that would be the wrong thing to do. Peter would just say he was creeping and do something to upset it. Like when Archer had offered to wash up the pots and pans after Sunday lunch. He was almost finished when Peter sneaked up and poured something dark and sticky all over them.

~*~

'What a mess. Still you've got nothing better to do than play at being a girl. I think you just like wearing me Mum's apron. Proper kinky that is.'

Archer had said nothing, rinsing each pan off quickly, but he was more wary and when Kyle tried it five minutes later he was ready for him, taking the bottle away before he could get anywhere near the sink.

'Julie, Archer's nicked my coke. He's a thief.'

She didn't respond immediately, she was fed up with the number of times they came running to her telling tales of Archer's supposed misdeeds. Her glance took in the puddles of liquid on the floor and drips running down the cupboard door of the sink unit. 'Get another bottle from the fridge and leave Archer alone. He's trying to help, that's more than the rest of you ever do.' Getting some kitchen roll, she wiped down the door and mopped up the spill on the floor. Straightening up, she took the meat tin off him and put it away. 'Is everything alright Archer? You would tell me if they were ... well, teasing you or anything. I know they can be a bit of a handful at times, but they're good boys really.'

He looked at her, seeing a woman who was doing her best to provide a good home for four of the most selfish individuals he had ever laid eyes on. She didn't deserve to be treated with such ingratitude for everything she did for them all day long: shopping, cooking, cleaning and washing. Her evenings and any spare minutes she got in the day were spent reading through other people's words, correcting them for the few extra pounds it brought in. 'Don't worry, it's nothing I can't handle.'

'You're a good boy. I'm glad you came here, you could teach them all a thing or two about, well about a lot of things. Did you finish that book I gave you?'

'Oliver Twist? Yes thank you. It was a bit dismal, but that was probably what it was like in those days.'

'Would you like another one?'

'I hope you don't mind, I borrowed one written by William Shakespeare. It has lots of dramas about people like Caesar and the Kings of England.'

'No of course I don't mind, you're welcome to anything on those shelves, it's nice to see them being appreciated. But Shakespeare's quite difficult to read. If you're struggling with any of it I have a book somewhere that tells the stories in modern speech.'

He thanked her, without saying that he was finding them far easier to read than anything else on her shelves.

~*~

He was grateful for the book now as he sat in back of the car, travelling at speeds that made him feel dizzy. The sight of the countryside flashing past so quickly made his stomach lurch, so he could not look out of the window. Peter was listening to music on a small device that seemed to be connected to his ears with black threads. Strange, tinny sounds were coming from it and he was continually jiggling his leg or tapping out rhythms on the car door. Occasionally he would hum or sing along to the words under his breath and once or twice he hit the air rapidly with both fists loosely clenched. The first time he did this Archer froze, thinking an attack was imminent, but Peter was totally absorbed in his own world and oblivious to the fact that he was in a car and there were other people around. When it happened again several seconds later Archer tuned into the sounds coming from the device and realised that he was pretending to hit drums like Doug in his favourite band Gaelic Sound. But he couldn't understand why Peter was hitting the air in front of his head, the drummers he knew all carried their drums.

Archer tried to focus back on his book. He was finding the plot a little confusing with plays within plays and the images of Gaelic Sound playing didn't help matters as they brought back memories of combat and victory and dancing with Kayleigh and Patricia.

Five

It was probably the best and worst day of Archer's life so far. The competition had been good, apart from the fact that he was up against his two best friends. He'd beaten Finn in the second round after an incredibly close first round, only one point in it. Fletch was on another team so they didn't meet until the semi final when he only lost by one point. The final round had been a straight vote between him and his biggest rival Edlyn, the boy who had tormented him for the previous five years. The girl's final was between Bethia, the soft-hearted, talented beauty that Fletch had finally claimed as his girlfriend and Patricia, the slightly scary, incredibly intelligent girl who was responsible for Archer's first real kiss.

It had been a hard-won victory, including some decidedly underhanded tactics by Edlyn, sabotaging the vote so that he beat Tybalt to the final. That, however, was trivial compared to his attempts to stir up trouble between Archer and Patrica, using poor Kayleigh to try and cause trouble between them. Luckily she was smart enough to see that she was being used and despite fancying Archer herself Kayleigh graciously relieved Archer of his obligation to jump the bonfire with her, but she was happy when he asked her to dance.

Despite the efforts of Patricia and her friend Chrisya to teach him the complex grapevine steps, Archer struggled through the dance with Kayleigh. Somehow it was easier with Patricia, she knew exactly what to do and he just had to mirror her moves or hold her hand as she spun. It meant that she spent quite a lot of time in his arms.

~*~

As he remembered the sensation, his cheeks heated up.

'Is it too hot in the back Archer? You could open a window.' Julie sounded concerned.

'No way, I'll freeze.' Peter glared at him and he shrugged at Julie hoping she would understand. After a worried look she turned back to listen to the radio.

Archer tried to return to his pleasant memories, but that all seemed long ago and far away now. He focussed on the book enjoying the spirit of the main female character, Katharine and Petruchio's outrageous swagger which reminded him of Doug with his eye for the ladies.

Julie turned round again. 'There's the Tor. If you look out of the front windscreen you'll see it.'

Archer peered out of the front of the car, but he had no idea what he was supposed to be looking for.

'There it is, stupid.' Peter pointed over to the right of where he was looking. 'Blimey, anyone would think he'd never been to Glastonbury before.'

Archer was about to say that he had been there before when Julie jumped in with, 'Don't be nasty Pete. Just because he hasn't seen things before doesn't make him stupid.'

'Don't get on at the lad, it's just an expression. Archer can stick up himself, he doesn't need you nannying him.'

'I wasn't nannying, just trying to make Pete see …'

'Whatever. Look, shut up now or I'll miss the turn and end up stuck in the traffic. Then there'll be trouble.'

Archer couldn't see Julie's face but he could tell from the way her shoulders slumped and her arms folded that she was unhappy about Dave's reaction. Unlike Peter, who seemed to grow somehow, taking up more room on the back seat, his movements becoming larger and the sounds louder. Archer was upset at being the cause of her distress, it seemed very unfair that Dave would take the boy's side against his wife. That sort of thing would never happen in his world, the parents always backed each other up and the children respected the fact that they were the ones with the experience and were therefore in charge.

It was just one more aspect of this world that he thought was strange and they all thought was normal. If Peter was put in his world he would no doubt find many of the things they did unusual. He whiled away the next ten minutes imagining all the things Peter would find to complain about in his world: daily chores, prayers and festivals, the food, clothes, transport – or lack of it, the list was endless. Probably the biggest problem for him would be the lack of electricity and everything that seemed to go with it: games and toys, TV or radio that was constantly on in every room, mobile phones and the many different ways of re-playing music that someone else had made. But mostly the simple act of clicking a switch and having the room fill with light.

As they approached Glastonbury the strange shaped mound got bigger and Archer followed its progress as it went in and out of his view. The lunchtime traffic was slow through the town and Julie suggested they should start looking for somewhere to eat.

'McDonalds,' said Peter. I bet you've never had a burger have you? Archer wants a burger too.'

'I was thinking of pub grub. The Butcher's in Street do a good steak.'

'But Dawn will have done a big meal, you know what she's like. A burger will do.'

'It won't be for hours. I can eat two meals in one day.'

'And it will be expensive for the four of us.'

'That's alright, I'll buy. You don't have to have starters and puddings and I'm sure they'll do a burger for the lads.' He met Archer's gaze in the rear-view mirror as his tone coaxed. 'What do you say boys? A poxy fast-food burger with thin watery chips or a mouth-watering, home-cooked quarter-pounder with spicy golden wedges and all the trimmings?'

Archer didn't need to say anything, Peter was making enough noise for both of them, but yet again he felt Julie had been outnumbered. Although he would like to give her his support, he honestly did prefer the idea of the second option, Dave had made it sound much more appealing. So he said nothing, but by the time they were back on the road again, Archer wished he had found the courage to give her his support.

Six

Julie was tight-lipped as Dave came back from the bar with four large glasses full of golden liquid and a glass of water with a slice of lemon in it for her. 'They hadn't got the flavoured stuff you like. I just got you tap water seein' as how you were worried about the price.' One of the glasses was already half empty and he picked it up and swallowed the rest of the liquid making loud gulping noises. He slammed the empty glass down on the table with a bang and showed his satisfaction with a loud belch. He cuffed Peter on the head in a friendly gesture, saying 'Mind your manners, Pete, you're supposed to apologise in front of a lady. By George I needed that.'

Julie sipped the water, her face wrinkling at the harsh taste. 'I take it that I'm driving the rest of the way.'

'No I'll be fine. There's only thirty miles to go and it's only a couple of pints, the food will absorb that. Unless you want to drive, then I can have another couple.'

'No that's fine, you drive.' She shuddered and Archer could tell that she didn't like the idea of him drinking.

'Come on Archer, drink up. That's real Somerset cider, the best in the land.' Dave was a whole pint happier.

'Maybe he's to pu… poncey to drink alcohol. Hey Dad, the pool table's free.'

'The food will be here soon.'

'Nonsense woman, they'll be ages. Come on lad.' Dave looked Archer as though trying to decide whether to include him. Although curious about the game, Archer felt it would be rude to leave Julie on her own and they left.

'You don't have to stay here. If you want to go and play pool, I wouldn't mind.'

'I wouldn't know what to do.'

'I'm sure they would show you.'

He kept his expression neutral. 'I'm sure they would.'

She looked at him intently, then a loud burst of laughter made her eyes flick over to the pool table. Archer looked over to see Dave with his arm round the waist of a serving girl, looking straight at Julie who was trying to smile.

'It's not what it looks like. He comes in here with his brother quite a lot, they all know him.'

Archer didn't say anything, but she obviously thought she could read his expression and tried to excuse him.

'He's a good man really. He tries to be a good husband and father, but right now he's under a lot of pressure at work. They always seem to be threatening to close the place down; they're laying people off every other month.'

'So he gets drunk to forget his problems.'

'Yes. No. Oh I don't know. I suppose it might help a bit. Don't the men drink where you come from? Or don't they have problems?'

'Yes they drink. And yes they have problems. But only the young men drink so much that they behave badly. Once they have children, men have to be responsible and stop behaving like children. Of course, when the children are grown they can go back to being foolish again.' He smiled thinking of some of the tricks played on Samhain when the ancients took great delight in pretending to terrorise the young children in scary masks.

'It sounds good. It must be good if all the young men are brought up with such a caring attitude as you.'

She patted his knee and Archer felt uncomfortable with her praise; he was ordinary, there were many who were better. He tried to think of something to distract her away from his world. 'So why is he drinking so much today?'

'He hates my family.' She looked shocked by her own words and tried to explain. 'No, that's not true, he doesn't hate them, he hates they way they live and the things they stand for. He calls them anal-retentive and goes on at great length about how stupid they are for thinking that any tiny little thing they do is ever going to save the planet.' She took a big gulp of water. 'I mean there are times when even I think they go too far, spending ages washing milk bottle tops and removing every last staple from magazines. But after talking to you it makes a lot more sense. If every person did their bit it would make a difference.'

A girl brought their food and the others appeared. Dave had almost finished his second pint and Pete was halfway through his, but Archer's was barely touched.

'Not enjoying the cider? Then you won't mind if I steal some.' Dave poured half of it into his own glass and Julie looked shocked, but Archer shrugged to show he didn't mind. 'That's a Snake Bite now, lager and cider. It's all we used to drink when we were your age. We thought we were really hard. Three of them and you'd be sick as a dog. Here, try some.'

He shoved the glass under Archer's nose and he took a sip, shuddering at the sour, bitter taste.

'Put hairs on your chest that will.'

Dave's description of the meal was an exaggeration, Julie's cooking was much better. Archer didn't see the point in shredding the beef into tiny strands then crushing them all together except to make it easier for infants to eat. The potatoes were cooked with their skins on, but dripping in unhealthy fat and covered in a stale red powder.

'Don't you like the wedges? I'll have them if you don't want them.' Peter saw him examining the red stuff and quickly speared a couple from Archer's plate with his fork, stuffing them in his mouth.

'I like them well enough, I was just wondering what the red powder was.'

'Some kind of spice,' Dave said with his mouth full. 'Julie will know. Too hot for you?'

'No, just an unusual taste.'

'I think it's paprika, you're not allergic are you?'

'Stop fussing Mum.' Peter's tone must have hurt.

Archer had to focus on something to redirect the anger that was boiling under his skin. He could not stomach the thought of putting anymore of the food that had been altered beyond recognition into his mouth. Pushing his plate away, he watched as Dave and Pete fought each other like crazed dogs, stabbing at each other's hands with forks. Julie's expression was pained and he was annoyed that she was suffering once more because of something he had done. He stood up abruptly. The chair leg caught on something and tilted back as though it was going to fall, but his quick reactions caught it before it made even more noise, preventing further embarrassment for Julie. She looked up. 'Are you alright? You look a bit peaky.'

'I'm fine, I just need some fresh air.'

'I'll come with you, I need the loo. It's on the way.'

He had given up trying to decipher all the strange euphemisms people used in this world when they needed to relive themselves or why they felt it necessary to announce the deed to those around. It was one of the few rituals they regularly performed, like blessing someone when they sneezed. As they reached the corridor to the toilets Julie put her hand on his arm.

'Are you sure you're alright? You looked quite angry in there. Try not to let them wind you up so much, I mean annoy you.' She had begun to translate the strange modern expressions automatically as soon as he looked a bit blank and sometimes even if he didn't. 'The more you react the more they will do it. That's how they get their kicks, I mean they enjoy it, it entertains them. I just ignore them now, it's the last thing they want.'

'Do you mean it doesn't wind you up any more?'

'No. Sometimes they can be quite cruel and it hurts, but I stopped letting them see how it affects me. Eventually I hope it won't affect me at all.'

She gave a small, sad shrug and turned away. Going outside, Archer took several deep breaths to calm himself down. Julie's explanation was similar to a trick he learnt many years ago when he was being tormented and attacked on a daily basis. With the help of his foster mother Ganieda and the specialist trainer Kalen who was skilled in many mental techniques, he learnt how to create a room in his mind where he could go when he didn't want to show his emotions to the outside world.

Seven

'No, stop. Please, I can't take any more.'

'You can and you will. Unless you can learn to stop reacting when someone is doing something to you that you don't want them to, the bullying will never stop.'

'Alright, I understand. I can do it, just please don't do that any more. I can't breathe.' Archer's voice was hoarse.

'I'm not going to stop as long as you continue to react. You can only make me stop by letting me know that you are no longer affected by it. If you stop breathing I will have to breathe for you. I think you can guess how unpleasant that would be.'

Archer had watched Kalen revive a child that had fallen from a horse and stopped breathing. It was uncomfortably close to a kiss, involving covering the child's mouth with his own. The thought sobered him and he grabbed a great gulp of air into his lungs, but it was no good, there was a searing pain and the tears ran down his cheeks. 'Please, just let me get my breath back and we can start again. No please, Kalen, just a minute, I beg you. Don't bring that thing near me … nooo!!!'

Archer's legs were stretched out a foot more than was comfortable and thick straps round his ankles bound them firmly in place. His feet and chest were bare, his only clothing was the normal wrestling attire: a pair of short, tight breeches which stopped above his knees. His arms were strapped to great iron rings so tightly that they were nearly pulled out of their sockets. The iron rings were set in concrete posts which stood three paces apart so the muscles on his bare torso were stretched taut. He felt uncomfortably vulnerable. As he buckled the leather cuffs round Archer's forearms, Kalen had done an excellent job of describing how this method of torture had been brought back from the Middle East where they would blindfold the victim and do unspeakable things to his body with knives and spears, rats and even honey and ants.

'You see, so much of the fear is in the mind. Some men died of sheer terror before a finger was ever laid upon them. Men who survived would only have to catch the scent of honey in the breeze or hear the scratch of a claw and they would be bringing back their dinners.'

'Surely not.'

'Surely yes. But to do that a man must have a great imagination. Take a look at this tray of instruments. How do you think they might be used to extract a confession?'

Archer looked at the evil looking array of bent and twisted hooks and blades, each sharpened to cruel looking points. There were three items he did not understand.

'Why is the fork there? I suppose you could use it to stab someone or pierce their kidney, but a spoon? That wouldn't cut anything.'

'It would if you dug hard enough, and it would hurt a lot more as well. Actually, that's just left over from dinner, they're not supposed to be there at all.'

'And the feather? How could you possibly hurt someone with a feather?'

Kalen picked it up and brandished it close to Archer's face, scratching down his cheek with the sharpened quill. 'Oh there are a number of places you could stick this where it would cause unimaginable pain. Underneath a fingernail, through a nostril, in the corner of an eye.' He lowered the feather to Archer's waist as though he was considering his belly button, then whispered in his ear. Archer's eyes grew wide as he mentioned various other places a feather could be used. Kalen hid the tray from view as he picked up and rejected several objects.

'So, do you think you are ready for this? I'll give you a bit of a chance the first time. I won't blindfold you so that you can see it coming, it's not quite so terrifying.' He brought his left hand forward and Archer knew without looking what was in it. 'You know the rules. I will not stop until you can convince me that your mind has complete control over your body. You can only do that by refusing to acknowledge the messages coming to your mind from your skin and muscles. Ready?'

Archer nodded, not trusting himself to speak as Kalen examined various sites on Archer's body as though deciding where to start. Each time he got close, Archer flinched before the feather even touched his skin. Kalen chuckled wickedly. When he stopped flinching at the threat of touch, Kalen actually touched him gently with a fingertip and it was like starting all over again as Archer learnt to resist the touch. Then, when he finally seemed to have controlled that, the real nasty stuff started.

Archer's scream had brought Niall running in, a look of impatience on his face. 'For goodness sake Archer, you can be heard all the way over on the quintain. I would have thought you were made of sterner stuff than that.'

'Please, Niall, make him stop, I need time to recover.'

'Nonsense. You need to be able to do this under the greatest of stress. Have you tried his ear?'

'Not yet, I was saving that, it doesn't get much worse. But I don't want him to damage his neck trying to resist.'

'Let me do it then. I love this bit.' Taking the feather from Kalen, he carefully got it into the right position just above the lobe and used a circular motion to tease and tickle all of the sensitive flesh around and inside the ear.

But Niall was denied his fun. It could have been the presence of one of the senior professors or his demanding physical instructor, both titles Niall could claim. Or the fact that while they were talking Archer had managed to regain some breath and with it some composure. Whatever it was, Archer now had his laughing reflex firmly under lock and key so that no matter what Niall did with the feather he remained immobile and impassive. He had reached what Kalen called "the cold face", a state of self control so strong that no words or deeds had any impact.

'Not bad on your first session. You won't do it next time.' Niall threw the feather down as though it was over.

'Yes I will.' Even as Archer spoke, he knew that it was a ruse, an attempt to crack his composure and sure enough, with no feather, Niall used his fingertips to tickle the sensitive flesh under Archer's arms and down his sides to waist level. This time, Archer was ready for him and did not so much as blink.

'Excellent. Well done. You can release him now.'

Eight

When Archer returned to the table, Dave had bought himself and Peter another round of drinks and they were playing a game of pool. Julie was sitting with one of her manuscripts, pencil in hand, concentrating on reading the words and shutting out everything else. He watched the game and quickly worked out that it was all about angles and forces. Peter was lining up the stick to hit the white ball so that it would knock the yellow ball into one of the end holes. Archer knew he hadn't quite got it right. 'You need to move an inch to the right.'

'What, you're some kind of expert are you? Dad tell him, he's trying to put me off my stroke.'

'No actually, he's right. Do as he says.' Peter grumbled as he moved it, and the ball trickled up to the pocket but didn't quite make it. Dave was in his element. 'Nice safety mate, that's going to make it a bit trickier for my next pot, but nothing I can't handle. Blue stripe, centre pocket.'

Archer quickly picked up on the terminology, the sticks were called cues, the white ball was the cue ball and the holes were pockets. The other balls were either stripes or spots and the first to pot the black was the winner. 'So you cannot hit any ball apart from the cue ball, is that right?'

'You never played before? Do you want a go?'

'No that's not fair, I don't want to watch.' Peter's good mood was rapidly dissolving into typical gloom.

'How about me and Archer against you then, that should balance it up a bit.' The beer made Dave uncommonly laid-back.

'Yeah ok, but I don't wanna break.'

Dave racked up the balls, explaining the way they were arranged in the wooden frame, alternating stripes and spots. He blasted the white ball into the corner of the triangle and the balls split apart bouncing off the sides, many of them clustering back together.

'That was nasty Dad, you've left me with nothing on.' Archer looked at him curiously, he was still wearing the same clothes.

'He means there aren't any balls waiting to be potted.'

'But they are just inanimate objects, they cannot wait.'

Dave was starting to get annoyed by the explanations, snapping 'It means none of them are covering the pockets.'

This didn't help, but Archer knew when to be silent. Peter tried to pot a stripe but got the angle wrong and it cannoned into the cluster sending three of the spots to cover pockets. Dave started lining up on one of them.

'Hey Dad, it's Archer's go.'

'I know, but he'll mess it up and then you'll get these three easy ones. He can go next time.'

'That's not fair. You said he could have a go.'

Archer couldn't decide why Peter was supporting him so enthusiastically, but he was still a little uncertain of the rules. 'So if I get the first ball in, then I can have a go at another one, is that right?'

'Exactly. That's why I want to take this shot, because I know I can do all three.'

'So when you hit the cue ball, you have to use the right amount of force so it will rebound into a good position for the next ball.'

'Yes, yes. You make it sound like a science lesson. Just get on with it.' Dave handed him the cue impatiently and Archer lined it up over the middle spot. 'Don't do that one or you'll never get the blue one in the corner pocket. Do the green first.'

Archer zoned everything out, hitting the ball with just enough force so that it potted the ball in the middle pocket and rebounded in a perfect position to pot the red.

'Beginner's luck,' grumbled Peter and Dave looked on in amazement as Archer potted four more spots and had one of the remaining two covering the middle pocket.

'Is there anything in the rules that says I cannot pot all seven balls and the black in a single go?'

'As if.' Peter snorted.

Dave examined the other spot, surrounded by three stripes. 'Yeah. The rule that says you're a lying cheating brat. Never played pool before. You've probably done nothing else all your short life. The rule that says you're a smug git, but a hell of a pool shark.' Despite his apparent anger, Dave was chuckling. 'No lad, there's no rule, but this ten pound note says you can't do it.' He put a tatty, scrunched up piece of paper on the ledge around the table.

Several people had realised something was going on and were crowding round, but it cost Archer no effort at all to exclude their fidgeting and whispers of disbelief. The automatic calculator in his mind was computing all the possible strategies, with precise angles and ball velocities and forces involved, even though he did not quite know them by these labels. Finally the way became clear, the sequence of shots and the final resting places of all the other balls played out in his head as though on a TV programme. There was just one thing missing. 'Do I have to pot the white ball after the black?'

'Yes,' said Peter, grinning. He got a cuff for his troubles.

'Take no notice of the lad, he's a sore loser. No. If there's any kind of foul on the black, he will win.'

'Ok.' Archer lined up on the ball in the cluster, ignoring Dave's advice to go for the other one first. He hit it with such force that it rebounded off two sides, knocking away the only stripe that was close to covering a pocket.

'Bad luck, mate,' said Peter, moving to the table. But Archer's shot was not finished yet. One of the stripes guarding the spot had rebounded with some force and was slowly trickling toward the other spot. 'Hold on.' Dave pulled him back and the watching crowd seemed to be waiting with bated breath as it kissed the spot which rolled to the edge of the pocket. It seemed to be having a protracted debate with itself about the pros and cons of actually making the jump into oblivion. A pin dropping would have been loud enough to break the tension in the room, but the vibrations set off by the massive round of cheers and stamping of feet did not actually begin until after the ball had chosen not to stay. Amidst the repetition of "in off" which rippled round the delighted crowd like a handshake at a reunion, Archer quietly potted the remaining spot and the black.

'Here son, this is yours and well deserved. I don't think I've ever seen that done in all my born days.' Dave handed him the crumpled note. 'I don't care if you are a ringer, that shot was amazing. It's like you'd actually calculated all the angles and speeds or something.' Even Peter seemed to have forgotten his hostility for a while, raising his hand in a "high-five" which was so like their own victory handclasp. 'Awesome, mate. Truly awesome. I can't wait to tell the others.'

Even Julie had forsaken her manuscript to come up and watch and she repeated Peter's 'Awesome.' Dave seemed to be taking full responsibility for the whole thing, claiming to have "taught him everything he knows". He was not happy about getting back in the car, but Julie insisted and he was in such a good mood because of all the attention that he finally agreed. Archer thought it strange that Dave could change between such different moods so quickly, one minute laughing and joking, the next minute angry and shouting. It was easy to see where Pete got it from, although he had an extra streak of meanness when he was with his friends.

Seeing him with his little cousins, Archer could easily believe there wasn't a mean bone in Peter's body. They obviously worshipped him as some kind of hero, but then Mikey was only five and Geena only three. Mikey had a toy sword and shield made of a smooth, flexible material Archer found out was called plastic. It seemed to have many different uses, but, like paper, it took a lot of energy and resources to create. The weapons looked authentic with intricate sculpted patterns, from a distance you may think they were real. It was an illusion, they were nothing like as solid as the wooden counterparts he played with as a child.

Mikey wanted to play rough games, pretending to fight like any boy of that age, and Geena wanted to be swung around in circles. When he stopped doing that she just wrapped herself around Peter's leg, making it difficult for him to defend himself against Mikey's attack. There was no doubt in Archer's mind that this was the real Peter, the boy he could be if he wasn't continually exposed to the ignorance, lack of respect and ingratitude of the males around him. Even as he was enjoying this carefree play Archer was attuned to potential danger, so he saw the accident building up long before it was anywhere close to happening.

Peter had turned his body and one of his legs to escape the battering but the other was firmly anchored where it was by the clinging Geena. Mikey ran in front and barged at him with his shield like a battering ram. Archer's warning shout came a split second too late as Peter began to fall. If the combined body weight of the two of them landing on Geena wasn't peril enough, her head would land exactly on the edge of a low tree stump.

Nine

Archer did the only thing he could think of doing, throwing himself at them from the other direction, bearing the brunt of their weight on his left shoulder. Somehow, he managed to simultaneously shield Geena's head against the impact and deflect her so that she would not be crushed by the impact of his and Peter's bodies. They all ended up in a tangle of limbs, but she had been thrown clear. She was badly shaken up and started crying, but Archer knew that she had no idea how much danger she had been in. He picked her up and dusted her down, then distracted her by making a big deal of how much her toy rabbit must be hurting and how brave he was not to cry.

That Peter knew exactly how much danger Geena was in was evident from his expression as he fell. He too was badly shaken and needed to release the reaction energy, but big boys don't cry so he did the only thing available to him, taking out his fear and frustration by shifting the blame. Mikey was so terrified that he couldn't cry until Peter shouted at him, at which point he howled even louder than Geena.

'Shut up you little runt, you'll have all the grown ups out and I'll get the blame.'

'No you won't Pete, it was an accident, nobody meant it to happen.'

'It doesn't matter, they'll still find a way to blame me, they always do. Shut up Mikey.'

'Mikey won't stop crying until you stop shouting at him. Tell you what, why don't we all run to the bottom of the field shouting as loudly as we can, then they'll think it was all just a game.' Archer picked up Geena and they both ran off shouting silly words like "sausages" and "rabbits". Mikey looked at Peter uncertainly as he rolled his finger round near his temple to indicate that Archer was mad, then followed suit, copying Geena by waving his arms around. Mikey copied everything Peter did and by the time they reached the hedge they were all laughing.

'You're a bloody nutcase you are, but you certainly seem to know your stuff with the little kids. Have you got any brothers or sisters?'

'No, but where I come from the older kids have to take a share in looking after the little ones, teaching them things and showing them the right way to behave.'

'Like a role model. That's what Mum's always saying to Dad, "You're not a good role model for Peter." Dad hates it. Says that's what we pay teachers for, to teach us how to behave.' It was the first time Peter had attempted anything like a decent conversation with Archer and as they took a slow walk back up the steep slope, he shyly opened up, asking questions about Archer's previous foster home and where he'd learnt how to play pool.

'That really was my first game. I'd never seen anything like it before today.'

'Well how did you work out the angles then? And how hard to hit it?'

'Like your Dad said, it's basic geometry and physics. You just need to balance things.'

'Sounds like equations. I'm poo at algebra.'

'You pooh at algebra? Doesn't that make a mess?'

Peter laughed, pretending to wipe the tears from his eyes. 'You can be such a dork sometimes. You need to start talking more like we do or the kids at our school are going to eat you for breakfast.'

'No. Really? I was reading about people like that in the encyclopaedia. Cabbilans or something.'

'Cabbi...oh, you mean cannibals. Can I give you a piece of advice if you want to survive in this town?'

'Sure, that would be most helpful.'

'Nah mate, you can't go round talking like something off a black and white movie. "That would be most helpful." That's so poncey you'll get called a pussy. And that is something you do NOT want.'

'A pussy is bad?' Archer frowned as the image of a fluffy white kitten scampered through his mind.

'A pussy is very bad. It doesn't get much worse than that. It's like being called a wimp or a wuss or a girl.'

'Ah we do that all the time. To someone who is weak or afraid, or just bad at sports.'

'Ok. Well look, if something is "most helpful", you say it's cool. Or sweet.'

'Got it. That's cool.'

'Good. Now here's the big piece of advice. If you don't know what something means or what it is, don't ask.'

'But I was always told you don't learn unless you ask.'

'I don't mean don't ever ask, I just mean don't ask in front of people you don't trust.'

'Like Jack and Kyle.'

'Exactly. You come over like a right dweeb, where in actual fact you're probably brighter than both of them.'

'Brighter? You mean I shine more?'

Peter laughed. 'What are we going to do with you? I mean smarter, cleverer. But I'm having my doubts.'

'So is a dweeb the same as a dork? Someone stupid?'

'Pretty much. More geeky than stupid.'

'Geeky?'

'My God, you really don't know nuffin' do you. A geek is someone with glasses and bad acne, scruffy hair and trousers that don't touch the floor.'

'That's about how they look, not how smart they are.'

'Oh they're usually quite clever, read lots of books, but they're not street smart. They're completely uncool.'

'So cool is something I want to be.'

'Definitely. Here endeth the lesson for today.'

'Just one thing.'

'What?'

'If I don't know nuffin', then I must know something.'

Peter pretended to scream. 'Stop that now or I'll throw something at you.'

'You'd miss, you throw like a girl.' Archer was off and running before he even finished the sentence and Peter chased after him. They arrived back at the house just as Julie and Dawn came round the corner.

'Where are the little ones? They need to come in and get washed up ready for dinner. Go and get them Pete.'

'Sure Mum.' He pointed at Archer. 'I'll get *you* later.'

'You'll have to run a lot faster than that to catch me.'

'Gosh Julie, what's happened to Peter?' Dawn seemed surprised. 'I haven't seen him this cheerful in ages. You must be having a good effect on him Archer.'

'Oh he certainly gives them a good example, he's always helping with the clearing up. He's the most thoughtful boy I've ever known.'

'Stop it, you're making him blush.'

'Nonsense. Everyone could use a bit of praise now and then. You seem to be getting on a lot better with Pete now Archer, is that right?' Julie looked happy and relaxed in her sister's company.

'Yeah, he's cool.'

'Good.' She smiled over at Peter who was holding his arms out like an aeroplane and running with his cousins either side of him, copying his moves. All three were making engine noises as loudly as they could.

The meal went well, the adults sat at one end of the table and kids on the other. Geena was proud that she didn't need a high chair any more but she kept wriggling about on her booster seat and it nearly fell off the chair. Dawn was jumpy with concern. 'Try to keep still or you'll have to sit next to me.'

'I felled.'

'No, you nearly fell.'

'I did fell. On the ground. But I didn't hurt. Bunny was hurt and Archer saved her.'

'What's this? You didn't say anything Peter.' Dave's tone was sharp, stopping all conversations round the table. All eyes were on Peter who was blushing to the tips of his ears.

Archer reached for a roll from the bread basket to distract their attention. 'There was nothing to say, it was an accident. Geena tripped and fell. I caught her but she dropped her toy. Nothing to worry about.'

'She nearly banged her head on the tree.' Mikey's voice piped up just as Pete's colour was returning to normal. Once more, Archer tried to defuse the situation with a normal tone of voice. 'But she didn't. Everyone was a bit shaken up so we ran down the hill to take away the fright energy. No-one was hurt so we didn't mention it.'

'My goodness, that was a smart thing to do. We were just lucky you were there to catch her.'

'Pete tried as well, but I was closer so I got there first.'

'A couple of heroes. Extra portions of pudding I think.'

'Yeah, well done Pete, Archer. I'm proud of you.' Dave's word's meant so much to Peter that Archer was glad he'd embellished the story a bit.

The new-found friendship continued throughout the evening as Peter introduced him to Monopoly; he was happy to show off his skill at the complex game. It made little sense to Archer, he struggled to adjust to the idea of paying rent to landlords and for services. There was nothing like that in his world; people built their own houses when they outgrew the family home. Peter was curious about the idea of living in a world where there was no electricity, bombarding Archer with questions about how they managed to do things without it. He also got into Julie's habit of explaining some of the expressions he used, every time he saw the blank look on Archer's face.

Archer was intrigued by the sleeping arrangements, Peter described it as a bunk bed and offered him the choice of sleeping on the top or bottom, even though it was quite clear to Archer that he would prefer the top bunk. 'I don't think I would like to sleep that far off the ground. What would happen if I turned in the night and fell? You have the top one.'

'Are you sure? It's got safety barriers. You must have seen a bunk bed before, Jack and Kyle have got one.'

'I've never been in their room. I bet Jack has the top one though.'

'How did you guess?'

'He does seem to rule the roost a bit.' It was Peter's turn to look blank. 'Like on a farm. All the hens look up to the rooster. Oh never mind. Like with a litter of puppies, one of them always has to be stronger and take the lead.'

'Like top dog.'

'Exactly. Jack seems to be top dog and the rest of you dance to his tune. Although you seem to be rivalling him just lately.'

Peter's face turned nearly as red as it had at dinner. 'I guess we were a bit mean to you, but it's what happens in foster homes. Survival of the fittest.'

'But you are not a foster child. They are your real parents.'

'You wouldn't think so sometimes.' Peter muttered it as he turned away, but Archer's sharp hearing picked up on it. Before he could say anything, there was a knock on the door and Julie came in, telling them that people were trying to get to sleep.

Ten

Breakfast the following morning was more like those Archer was used to, a proper family affair with everyone sitting together and helping themselves from plates piled with bacon, sausages, fluffy yellow eggs, mushrooms, tomatoes, beans and triangular potato shapes Dawn called hash browns. 'Sorry there's no fried potatoes, but I was up late. Chestnut was up all night with colic, I was trying to move it on. He's been nibbling at the green hay again, I can't keep him away from it no matter what I do.'

'Have you tried rubbing his belly with …'

'You name it, I've rubbed it.'

'What about chamomile, valerian and peppermint broth?'

'Really? I haven't had much success getting him to drink anything.'

'Add some sweet cicely or lady's mantle and he won't be able to resist. Make sure it's blood heat, but no more.'

'Sounds good, I might try that later. Do you ride then?'

'A bit. I'm not very good.'

'What there's something you can't do well? Never.' Pete grinned to show he was only joking.

'I was going to ask Pete to take the two mares out for a bit of exercise. The stable girl has rung in sick and I'm all behind. If you two take them it would be a big help, you could do the longer route.'

'Sure, we'd love to, wouldn't we Archer?'

'Yeah, I'd be happy to help, but you must let us clear the table and wash up first.'

Peter did not look happy to do this, but Archer made a game of it with the phrases he learnt yesterday. Pete would say a word or phrase and Archer had to use it in a sentence, then Peter had to think of a synonym using the same sentence. It got very silly, with Peter deliberately giving false translations but it passed the time quickly and before Pete realised it, the job was done.

'That wasn't so bad was it?'

'What, you saying Jack is not as bright as the kitchen light? It's probably true, at least the light knows how to shine when you switch it on.'

'No, I meant helping out in the kitchen. If you do it with a mate and have a bit of fun …'

'Sorry, but coming from a sixteen-year-old boy that is just too weird. It's the sort of thing my Mum would say. Or Aunty Dawn. You're not telling me that boys are like that where you come from. Do you all do this "whistle while you work" routine?'

Archer's face hardened. 'Either you do your share of the work or you don't get your share of the food. It's that simple. If everyone does their bit, it doesn't take long and yeah, we do try to have some fun to make it less tedious.'

'Well I get it, but it doesn't make me want to do it. I'm only a kid and that's what grown ups are for. I'm just supposed to go to school and learn things, that's my job.'

'Don't forget about making your Mum's life a misery.'

'Absolutely. Dad too. If they didn't want to do things for me they shouldn't have had me.'

Archer didn't want to risk breaking their tenuous bond by suggesting that Peter was being selfish. If the TV shows were anything to go on, he was just being a normal teenager. He shrugged and let it go as they went to find Dawn. She was so pleased with the job they'd done she gave them a chocolate bar, saying she'd meet them by the stables in ten minutes.

Archer munched happily as they wandered down. 'See, you wouldn't have got that if you hadn't helped.'

'Big deal. If you think a mouldy old chocolate bar is going to make me offer to wash up at home, you can think again. The others would completely take the piss out of me. Anyway, I know where Mum keeps them, I can have one whenever I want.'

'You would take one without asking? That's stealing.'

'How is it? It's my house and she buys them for me, so how can it be stealing?'

Archer didn't have an answer for this, so he changed the subject. 'That sounds painful.'

'What does?'

'Completely taking the piss out of you. Do they have a machine for doing that? Some kind of pump?'

'No, it's an expression. It means … you know what it means, you were making fun of me.'

'No, I was taking the piss.' Archer anticipated that Pete would react violently and dodged the friendly slap, almost running into Dawn.

'Right you two, we don't want that kind of horse play round the horses, they'll get the wrong idea.'

Peter was behind her and spun his finger round at his temple. 'Thank you Pete, but I'm not crazy and yes I have got eyes in the back of my head and I do know exactly what you're thinking. At all times.'

Peter's face was the picture of bewilderment and Archer grinned, he had heard Ganieda say something almost identical. He listened as Dawn ran down a list of dos and don'ts and gave them both helmets, but Pete groaned. 'Do we have to wear these things? I hate them.'

'Of course you do if you want to ride a horse, it's for safety. I bet you always wear a helmet don't you Archer?'

'Actually no. We don't have them.'

'Well you're not going out without them, I'll just have to call one of the other girls...'

'No it's ok, we'll wear them. Look, you have to do the straps up like this.'

Archer was surprised at Peter's change of attitude, but when he put the helmet on he understood his reluctance. It felt really uncomfortable and it looked strange on Peter. 'Do I look like a dweeb in this?'

'Oh yes. A proper geeky dork.' Peter smiled back, enjoying the joke.

'When you two have finished speaking Klingon, or whatever it is, I want you back here in forty minutes, you mustn't keep them out too long.'

Riding with Peter felt similar to when Archer was out with Fletch or Finn, with the same hint of competition. They were quite sedate at the start until they were out of sight of the stables. Peter immediately took his helmet off and seemed surprised that Archer had beaten him to it. 'I thought you'd be all goody-goody and do as you were told.'

'Just because I believe in helping out and studying hard doesn't mean I have to follow all their rules. The only time I wear a helmet on horseback is in the joust.' Archer hooked the helmet strap onto the saddle.

'You do jousting? Like in knights in shining armour?'

'Yeah we have to wear full armour. We train on the quintain without armour and we're not allowed on the tilt until the last year of juniors.'

'What at age ten? Isn't that a bit young?'

'No, fifteen. We start seniors at sixteen.'

'I've heard of those medieval re-enactments. Dad promised to take us to one at Warwick Castle, but he never did. What do you train on? A quinter?'

'A quintain. It's a post with a big wooden arm on it. One end has a shield which you hit with the lance. A bag filled with sand on the other end swings round and tries to knock you off. You need to be quick enough to duck or strong enough to resist it.'

'Sounds like fun.'

'It is. Except when you do get knocked off. Landing on the ground in armour is not my idea of fun and you have to get all the dents knocked out.'

'Which you have to do all the time.'

'Only the first time, when I was in a padded …' Archer realised that he was winding him up and smiled. 'I'm sure you would be falling every time if you tried.'

'Rubbish. I'm a proper horseman, me. Watch.' He tapped his foot on the mare's flank and she seemed to know what he wanted instinctively, speeding into a gallop in an instant. He raced across the fields, pulling up at the edge of a small thicket. He was quite impressive, but nowhere near as good as Finn, or even Fletch, but then they rode almost daily whereas Peter probably only got to do it when they visited the farm. Archer followed at a slower pace, it was unfamiliar terrain and he needed to get to know his mount before allowing her free rein.

'You wouldn't stand a chance against me in a race.'

'Not on this mare, but on Apollo, it would be different.'

'You've got your own horse? I thought you lived with foster parents. They must be loaded.'

'Loaded with what?'

'Dosh. Spondulicks. Money. They must be rich.'

'Are Dawn and Phil rich?'

'No, but they own a farm, so they have horses.'

'As did Sed … my foster parents.' They dismounted and led the horses to a patch of grass, tethering them to a tree and sitting down.

'It sounds really different where you come from, more like it was in my grandad's time. The way he goes on, its almost like Victorian times when they sent children up chimneys to sweep them. He's always saying how they had to help out and how easy we have it today.'

'And you don't think you do?'

'No. We're under a lot of pressure to do well all the time at school and there's all the homework. And every club you go to expects you to train three or four times a week and enter competitions and stuff.'

'Club?'

'Group of people. Like a rugby club or a football club.'

'A sporting association?'

'Exactly. I was in a swimming club for a while but they wanted me to start going before school. Sod that for a game of soldiers, I have to get up far too early as it is.'

'We usually get up when the sun rises. That can be four in the morning at midsummer.'

'That's manic. Mad. Crazy. Why would you do that?'

'There's always lots to do. Everything's growing really fast and the crops need tending…'

'Yeah, I suppose if you live on a farm. Dawn and Phil are a bit like that. Not quite sunrise though.'

'Well we do take an hour to get ready and have a big breakfast before we start.'

'I couldn't eat at that time in the morning, the idea makes me feel sick. And you have to eat an hour before you swim, so I would have to get up at five. No way. So then I tried the Ai-Ki-Do club for a while.'

'Ai-Ki-Do?'

'It's a martial art like Judo or Karate. Unarmed combat. Fighting without weapons.'

'We do that to improve balance and speed before…'

'Oh my God, look at the time, we've only got ten minutes to get back.'

They mounted up and galloped like their lives depended on it. Archer was holding back slightly, but as they came to the last field, his sharp eyes caught a flash of pink. It was Geena, standing right in the path of Peter's horse playing with her rabbit. Archer shouted at Peter, but he just looked back and grinned, caught up in the exhilaration of the chase. Some of Archer's desperate need communicated itself to his mare as he spurred her on.

Flattening her ears and lowering her head slightly, she forged ahead, catching up to Peter, but he just took it as a greater challenge and sped up even more. Archer pointed ahead, but Peter was in the blood frenzy brought on by battle and just laughed.

Archer brought his brave mare closer and closer until he could touch the front flank of Peter's mare, hoping to swerve her off course. Peter looked over in anger, but he must have caught sight of the pink. His expression changed to shock, then a kind of desperate horror as he tried to pull on the reins and swerve round her. Geena had finally heard the noise and turned round to see what was making it. She stood rooted to the spot, holding her toy rabbit out in front as though that would protect her.

Eleven

Archer knew that Peter could not make it, so with a prayer to Hengist, he attempted something he had only ever seen Finn pull off. He communicated his request to the mare through the pressure from his knees and she responded instantly, moving out enough so that he could lean over and scoop up the girl, holding her in his lap as he slowed the mare down to a gentle trot.

'Is she ok? Geena, how are you?' Peter looked as though he wanted to throw back his breakfast.

'That was fun. Do it again?' She had lost any sense of fear and was smiling happily.

'I don't think that would be a good idea. The horses are tired, they need to rest now. Come on, you can ride with me back to the stable.'

'But I want Petey to pick me up like you did. It was fun.' If she had been standing, she would have stamped her foot and Archer knew she wouldn't let it drop.

'Ok. I'll put you down and Pete can pick you up.' He looked over to check that he was recovered enough to do this, and Peter nodded his approval. They took the horses back and earned the job of grooming them.

'That's three times you've saved my bacon. Why would you do that after I've been so rotten to you?'

'I thought we only had bacon at breakfast and I didn't save you any.'

'This is getting silly; I'm having to explain almost everything to you. It means you got me out trouble. Like when you stopped me falling on Geena and crushing her.'

'But it wasn't your fault.'

'They still would have blamed me. Didn't you see them turn on me at the table? And you did it again, telling them I tried to save her, my Dad was well chuffed. I don't think he's ever said he was proud of me before.'

'I'm sure he must have done. When you get good marks at school or show him something you've made.'

'I never get good marks, I'm in the bottom set for everything. And I've never made anything.'

'Really?'

Peter shifted uncomfortably. 'I made some biscuits in food tech, but we ate them all before he came home.'

'Don't you learn any crafts like working with wood?'

'Yeah but whatever you make, the other lads wreck it, so I just leave it at school. I made a clock and the tech teacher kept it on her wall. She said it was really good.'

'Didn't your Dad see it when he visited the school?'

He snorted. 'As if. Dad hated school and he said that if he ever has to go in because I'm in trouble I'll get grounded for a year.'

'That's a shame. Sedge is a carpenter and he shows me things. I love carving wood. I made that bow.'

'You're kidding. Really?'

'Yeah. I went to see a man who showed me how to make bows. I worked for him over the summer and he gave me two yew staves to make my own bows.'

'Where's the other one?'

'There was an accident. No it wasn't. Edl - an enemy of mine stole her and threw her on the Beltane bonfire.'

'Beltane?'

'It's the May Day feast. We all choose a Worthy character and have a competition to see who gets crowned King and Queen of the May. I was Robin Hood.'

'Figures. I suppose you won?'

'Yes, but it was really close.' Archer turned away.

'So do you give your bows names then like people do with their cars?'

'What? Why do you say that?'

'You called your other bow her. You said he stole her.'

Archer was gripped by the powerful image of the nymph that had possessed his Bow. A powerful sprite that wanted her revenge on Edlyn for his mistreatment of the tree she had been cut from. He blushed as she remembered the image of the beautiful girl she had become in his mind. 'She was very curvy. Like a girl.'

Peter laughed. 'I don't think it's some old bow's got you blushing like that. There's a girl isn't there?'

'Three actually. Unless you count Bethia, but I had to kiss her, she was the May Queen.'

'You kissed four girls?' Peter was both horrified and fascinated, but he had no chance to find out more as Dawn appeared with a request.

'I know you've been really helpful already today, but I need to ask another favour.'

'Will there be more chocolate?' Archer had developed a real taste for it.

'Certainly. We need to get the dinner ready …'

'Oh no. I draw the line at peeling spuds.' Peter's face showed his horror at the idea.

'Well the alternative is keeping Mikey and Geena occupied. You did such a good job yesterday. Maybe you could take them for a walk or pick some fruit for pudding.'

'Aren't we having treacle tart and custard?'

'That's a winter pudding. The strawberries and some of the raspberries are ready. With ice cream or cream. Remember, don't pick them unless they're coming away in your hand.'

Phil insisted that the men should do the clearing and washing up after the meal. When Peter tried to explain that they'd already washed up once, Dave held up his palm saying he didn't want any excuses. This put Peter in a black mood and he plugged his headphones in and dried up sulkily, slamming each piece of cutlery into the drawer with a great crash until Dave cuffed him round the head.

It put a damper on the whole day, he was turning back into the sulky withdrawn boy he had been at home. Archer wondered if this was the pattern every time Peter tried to do something different, that his Dad would find something to criticise so he didn't bother trying to improve.

On the way home, as they reached Glastonbury, Julie asked if the boys wanted to have a walk up the Tor. 'I'd like to spend some time at the Well, and the walk will do you good after that huge meal.'

'And what am I supposed to do? I ain't going round no poxy prayer place.'

'You can go with the boys or sleep in the car. Failing that I'm sure you can find a pub open. If I'm driving, I get to choose when I take a break and that is now.'

'Alright, keep your shirt on. There's a pub on the main road opposite that well place. You can come and get me when you're ready.'

They parked on a side street and as they walked, Julie explained to Archer about the Chalice Well, a living sanctuary where water flowed at the same rate and temperature all year round. 'The water is supposed to have healing properties and wherever it flows, turns red. They say it's the blood of Christ from where the Holy Grail was buried or something. I just love the peace and quiet of the beautiful gardens. I like to pop in here every time I'm passing by, it gives me a real lift.'

'That sounds good.' Archer had drunk from that same well in his world. He had to be very careful what he said, it was best to say nothing about these things at all, which meant that he was constantly on his guard. It was never more necessary than when they reached the top of the mound. The tower at the top looked different to the one he knew and he read the notice saying that the original St Michael's church was destroyed in an earthquake in 1275 and was rebuilt in 1360. It had been fallen into ruin after 1539 when the monasteries were destroyed. When he stood inside and looked up it was just a great shell, almost impossible to climb. Almost, but not quite. Peter was looking at him with interest, he'd actually taken the ear-pieces out.

'You're not thinking you could climb that are you?'

'Maybe not today with all these people around, but if you got up early enough …'

'You really are bonkers aren't you? Tell me, what did it feel like when you kissed the girl?'

'Which one?'

'Any of them. How come there were so many?'

Archer shrugged. 'I was the May King. It's supposed to be good luck to kiss him.'

'And you had to kiss the May Queen.'

'In front of the whole village. But worse, in front of her boyfriend Fletch who just happens to be my best mate.'

'Was she a dog? I mean, you know, ugly or fat.'

Archer brought up a picture in his mind of her blonde perfection and slender curves. He shook his head. 'Just about the prettiest girl in the village. Long blonde curls, huge blue eyes, curves in all the right places.'

Peter grinned. 'I know the type. An absolute bitch, full of herself and nasty to lesser mortals. One of the popular crowd that rules the roost as you would say.'

'Not at all. I thought exactly the same at the start, couldn't see what Fletch and Finn were drooling over. But I spent the afternoon watching her be kind, generous and really sweet.' He shrugged.

'So you fancy her as well. That's tough. Maybe she'll like you more because you won that competition thing. Was she a good kisser?'

'I don't know. She was the first girl I ever kissed, I had nothing to compare it to.'

This was obviously a topic that Peter was keen to explore in some depth as he just wouldn't let it drop. 'Come on Archer, tell me more, what was it like?'

'I really can't say, it all happened so quickly.'

'You must have felt something. Try and remember, it's important.'

With a sigh, Archer closed his eyes and went back to that never-ending minute where he worried that Fletch would never speak to him. Then his lips had met Bethia's briefly. 'Warm, soft, she tasted of honey.'

Peter let out his breath. 'Is that it? Didn't you, well didn't you *feel* something? Like inside?'

'Not with Bethia, no. But it was just a quick touch.'

'Aha, what about the others?'

Sensing that there was more to this than idle curiosity and resolving that he would more than get his revenge shortly, Archer accessed the collection of sensations stored in the "kiss" box in his memory. 'Kayleigh was clumsy and our noses knocked together first. Chrisya tasted of strawberries, she was an expert, holding my face for ages. The rest were just shy little pecks on the cheek.'

'Except?'

'Except nothing. That's it.'

'Bullshit. You're holding out on me. One of them was special, the one you fancy. She was different to the rest.'

Archer did not want to discuss Patricia's kiss with anyone, it was something private and wonderful and even now as he thought about it, his heart began to race and he began to feel warm and prickly.

'I knew it. Did you get a funny feeling inside, like your guts were twisting up and your heart wanted to explode?'

'Well you obviously did. Who is she?'

Peter realised he'd given himself away and blushed. 'We need to be getting back now, Mum will be wondering where we are.'

'She knows where we are. She said an hour, it's only been half that. Come on, be fair. I told you everything, now you have to tell me.'

'No I can't. She'll kill me. She's going out with someone else.'

'Either you tell me or you climb the tower. Your choice.'

'You're not supposed to, we'll get into trouble.'

'Since when did that stop you? There are no notices saying you can't and there's no-one around now. Come on, you have to pay the forfeit.'

'I can't.'

'Because you have no arms or legs? There is no such word as can't, that's what Kalen always says. What you mean is you won't because you're a coward.'

'I am not a coward.'

'You're a girl then. No that's not fair; many of the girls I know would climb this.' Archer leapt onto the bench and found hand and foot holds to get him up to the first window ledge. He swung himself up and sat there confidently, folding his arms. 'See how easy it is? I bet Mikey could do it. Come on, I'll give you a hand.' He stood up and overbalanced, starting to topple. Peter screamed like a girl.

Twelve

Archer was in full control as he grabbed the window frame, he had only been messing around. He had a hunch about Peter's reluctance and wanted to test it out. It wasn't that he was cowardly, he obviously had some kind of fear of heights. Yet he had climbed to the top of the Tor without comment. He replayed their time at the top, realising that Peter hadn't been the slightest bit interested in looking at any of the views, spending the whole time looking at the ground, the tower or at Archer. He abandoned his plan of climbing to the top and let himself down slowly until he could leap onto the bench. He sat next to Peter who was as white as a sheet with a sick look on his face. The floor of the tower was rank with molten cow dung, that could not have been helping.

'Come on mate, let's get you out of here, it stinks.'

'No, just leave me alone. You were right. I'm a stupid rotten coward and a bully and I hate myself.'

'Bullshit. Or maybe it should be cowshit. There's plenty of it around here.' Peter gave a weak smile at the weak joke. The fact that Archer had actually sworn for the very first time made him take notice and he allowed Archer to help him out and they sat on the concrete platform with their backs against the tower. 'Why didn't you say you hated heights? I would never have come up here if I'd known and I'm sure your Mum wouldn't have suggested it if she knew.'

'I don't think it's a proper fear of heights, more a fear of falling. It's hard to explain.'

'Try. What's the difference?'

'Well I was alright coming up and I don't mind looking out at views like this as long as I'm sitting down or on solid ground. But I couldn't go near the edge and the thought of climbing that tower makes me want to vomit.'

'Even the thought of me climbing it made you feel ill.'

'Yeah. It happens sometimes when I stand at the top of a flight of stairs. I get this image of myself falling down, going over and over and my head goes all funny. The stairs start to wobble and I feel sick and I have to sit down 'til the feeling goes away. Then I'm late for class and I get into trouble.'

Archer was starting to realise how the bad things in Peter's life were causing him to behave the way he did. 'So how were you going to get down from here? All those stairs and having to look down all the time?'

'I don't know. I didn't think that far ahead. I just didn't want to look like a wuss in front of you or …'

'Or your Dad. His opinion means a lot doesn't it?'

'Of course it does. He's my Dad. But he thinks I'm rubbish. I bet he would be a lot happier if I was more like you – or if you were his son. He's always going on about how brainy you are. And Mum thinks you're wonderful because you help her so much.'

'That's only because it was the way I was brought up. I'm sure if I lived here all my life I'd be exactly like you.'

'No way. You've always got your head in a book.'

'Only because I want to learn about your life. If I lived here I'd already know wouldn't I? Look, we need to get back now, but I want you to try something for me.' They stood up and started walking down the long slope with Archer slightly in front.

'You're not going to tell me to close my eyes or walk backwards, I've tried all that.'

'No, this is part of our warrior training. If you have some kind of irrational fear, you need to fight it.'

'That's easy to say.'

'Nothing worthwhile happens without some effort on your part. What's your favourite thing in the world to do?'

'I dunno. I suppose it's playing Final Fantasy on the Nintendo. Or my skateboard, yeah, my skateboard.'

Archer had seen him on it, he was quite fearless. 'And how long did it take you to learn that?'

'I dunno. A couple of minutes just to get my balance.'

'But how long to do all the tricks?'

'Hours. Weeks. I had to build up to it. Especially the ramp at the park, that was really scary.'

'So this is the same. You have to take it a step at a time. If you start feeling weird or your eyes go funny, try not to focus on looking down all the time. Look up slightly or look to the side.' They had gone down the first set of steps and had reached a tight, curving staircase, each concrete step edged with wood.

'Whoa, it's happening.' Peter stopped and put his arms out to balance himself.

'Alright. Take a deep breath. Relax. Get into a rhythm with the steps, that will help. If your body is moving smoothly, your brain won't have so much to complain about.' He took one hand and pulled slightly but Peter's brain was not ready to let his body function.

'Tell me about this girl you kissed. You don't need to say her name, just tell me what she looks like.'

'Tall, for a girl. And skinny, she plays a lot of sports so she's well fit. Short brown hair with a blonde fringe and blond bits at the side.' He demonstrated with his hands, not realising that he was actually walking down the staircase now. Archer's diversionary tactic had worked. 'Big brown eyes, but she wears too much make-up and it spoils them. She's dead lippy to the teachers, they all think she's a right hard case, but she's not really, she just has a hard time at home. Her Dad's always calling her stupid.'

'Sounds familiar.'

'And her step-mum doesn't wanna know, she's got a baby.'

'I thought you said she's got a boyfriend. How do you know all these things about her?'

'She has. But he's using her. He just wants to be seen with the fittest girl in the year.'

'And you don't?'

'No. Well yes, obviously, but it's not like that. I've fancied her since year seven when she had frizzy hair and braces and loads of puppy fat.'

'Sounds appealing.'

'She was. Cute and cuddly and always laughing. Then her Mum died and she was off for ages. When she came back after the holidays she was like a different girl.'

'But you still like her?'

'Of course. You'll know why when you meet her. How come you're not going to school?'

'It's not worth it for two weeks. I've been given some tasks to study and I'll start in the new year in September.'

They were down past the high levels and the stairs had become long and shallow, presenting no problem and Peter was even able to run on the last section. He carried on running round the corner and up to the entrance of the gardens as Julie was just coming out.

It took longer to get back as there was a lot of traffic on the narrow roads, people making their way home from a day in the sun. The evening meal was quiet, Dave was still subdued after sleeping most of the journey back and the other two had not yet returned from their friend's house. Peter and Archer gave Julie a hand setting the table and clearing up afterwards but as soon as they heard the front door, Peter dropped the cloth and went to meet the other two and they all went out to the den. It was built as a garage originally, but was too narrow for a car so Dave had converted it into a games room for the lads. Archer wasn't invited, so he went up to his room.

Closing the door, he knew straight away that something was different. Someone had been in his room. You couldn't tell by looking, everything looked exactly as he had left it. There wasn't much in the room apart from the bed, just a small desk and chair and a wardrobe which fitted all the way across the shortest wall with a set of drawers, shelves of different sizes and space for hanging clothes. Archer could never imagine owning enough clothes to fill that much space, but some of the room was taken up with spare bedding.

The books on the shelves above the desk were still lined up in the order of their height but at least two of them were in different places. The model cars on the bottom shelf were mostly in the same order but the position of the two red cars had been swapped. So without doing any more, he knew that his privacy had been violated. Which meant that someone had either got a key for the lock or come in through the window. His first thought was that the other boys had come in to get his bow and he bent down and felt under the bed to check. It wasn't where he left it.

Thirteen

How could they have got into his room? They had been staying with a friend all the time he had been away and the door was locked. Resisting the urge to confront them, Archer sat cross legged and drew calming breaths, letting his warrior brain take over and assess the information. Kalen recently introduced him to a sophisticated technique that he would normally be learning as a senior and this was the perfect opportunity to practise it.

He learnt that every event, no matter how inconsequential, leaves an imprint. Just as minuscule specks of matter such as hairs, fibres and the oils in fingerprints are left behind, so are microscopic particles such as skin cells, droplets of sweat and even the residual energy from an action or thought. With the gift of heightened senses, some people can tune into an environment and detect events that had happened.

~*~

'Close your eyes and tell me what you can smell.'

'The flowers in the vase and my sweat. I could use a bath. And you, but not as strongly.'

'Good. Not bad for a start. Now that you have identified those smells, I want you to remember them and move past them. Can you smell anything else?'

'The chalk dust. The herbal tea gone cold, was it chamomile? The horse dung outside the window.'

'I think you're just expecting to smell that, I'm sure it would have been cleared up since this morning. And it was chamomile. Anything else?'

71

'An apple core in the bin. Leather covering the books.'

'Superb. Can you tell me what I had for lunch?'

'Apart from the apple? No wait, that was yesterday. Cheese, bread, no butter and some spiced tomato sauce.'

'That is truly amazing. You could really smell all that?'

'No, I cheated. It's what you have most days, I've seen you eating it. I had to choose between cheese or meat.'

Kalen chuckled. 'Well there's nothing wrong with your powers of observation or memory, but if you practice with this, sharpening your sense of smell, you should be able to distinguish between the scents left behind by a number of people. Have you ever walked down a corridor and known that Professor Gail was there a little while earlier?'

Archer nodded. 'Yes. Lavender and thyme.'

'If you were to develop this skill fully, you would no longer be able to stay in a room with her. She is rather liberal with it. The principle is the same, you can detect a person's presence several hours or even days later if you are familiar with their particular combination of aromas.'

'But doesn't it fade out after a while?'

'Of course. That's why it is so important to try not to disturb the air in the room, always smell and touch first. If you can, try to touch things with your tongue. It will help you to make a more detailed comparison because there is a big connection between taste and smell.'

Kalen explained that the woman who trained him had highly developed gifts. Her abilities were so advanced that she could hear snatches of conversations that had taken place in a room and even hear thoughts.

~*~

Archer tuned out the obvious smells in the room: his own familiar scent, the detergents used to wash the bed coverings and the slightly woody smell coming from the carpet. Then the pungent aroma coming from the oils on his bow, combined with the wood. He discounted all of these and examined what was left. There was definitely another sweaty smell in there, possible even two. They must have got in, searched under the bed and taken his bow out, then put it back the wrong way, with his insignia on the left instead of right. He checked the hiding place of his quiver, well hidden behind a panel at the base of the wardrobe and the tell-tale chocolate wrapper had moved.

Scratches round the front plate of the lock showed him their method of entry. Now that they had access to his room and knew where he kept the bow and quiver, they would be waiting for an opportunity to use it against him. The first question was, would it be better for him to re-hide things, letting them know that he knew, or should he accept that they weren't going to give up until they had tried? The second was, would Peter still be keen to help them after what had happened at the weekend?

There was an old saying that forewarned is forearmed, but there was not much Archer could do if they set upon him as before. Not that he couldn't handle all three, they were ignorant of basic techniques like neutralising an opponent with the minimum of energy. They were all brute force and ignorance, lashing out with fists and reacting to threat, relying on superior numbers to overwhelm resistance. If he wanted to, he could have disabled each one in turn with a well-placed punch or kick, but that would increase their determination to continue until they could best him.

Ancient military history taught him that an effective strategy was to divide and conquer and his study of recent military campaigns introduced him to the idea of "hearts and minds". He had gone some way toward winning Peter over to his point of view although he probably wouldn't yet have the resolve to stand up against the other two. It was obvious that Kyle was nothing more than a foot soldier, he would follow wherever Jack led. So Archer's main task was to convince Jack that he would never win in a contest of strength or wits. An idea began to form.

Saturday morning was the obvious time for action, Dave worked until lunch and Julie and always spent a couple of hours at the local market. If Archer had been planning the campaign, he would know that his adversary knew this, and it would have been the last time he would choose. These boys had little knowledge of principles such as logical anticipation and surprise or the modern warfare technique of multiple scenario modelling. So although he was fairly convinced that they would not strike during the week, he did not let down his guard. He spent most of the time in his room apart from meal times so that they would have no further opportunity to invade his territory.

There were elements of good strategy, if that was what it was. When their paths crossed, all three boys seemed to be slightly friendlier toward him, particularly Peter. If it wasn't for the discovery of the moved bow, Archer might have been fooled into thinking that he now felt a genuine friendship. When the other two weren't around, Peter relaxed back into the warmth and camaraderie they had shared at the farm and on the Tor.

Archer was more than ready for the betrayal when it came. Just as Edlyn had used Patricia to entice him to the yew forest, Peter was to be the lure to his undoing. Except that Patricia had been completely innocent and he nearly lost her friendship when he blamed her for her part in the deception. Well there would be no such mistake this time.

'Leave this Mum, we'll clear up, won't we boys?'

'Thank you Pete, I am running a bit late. I don't usually have all of you up on a Saturday morning for breakfast. You don't normally surface until lunch.'

'Must be the good effect Archer's having on us Mrs Reid. We'll have this place shipshape for when you get back. Me and Kyle are going to Brett's again.'

'Will you be back for lunch?'

'Not sure yet, depends how it goes. Probably not, but we will definitely be back for tea.'

'Peter would you and Archer mind making yourself a sandwich or something? Your Dad said he'd be late today so I can pop in on Cath and the new baby.'

'Take your time, Mum. We can manage without you for a few hours, you should take a break.'

'Thanks Pete, what a lovely thing to say.'

If he didn't know where all this was coming from, Archer would have been pleased with the small impact he had made on Peter's attitude to his mother. He watched her instinct to show gratitude with a hug over-ridden by the knowledge that Peter would shrug it off in front of the other boys. In the end she just patted his shoulder, completely oblivious to the undercurrents of scheming going on in three of the minds sitting round that table.

He was surprised when they kept their word and helped with the clearing up, he had expected them to disappear as soon as she left. It must be part of their plan to lull him into a false sense of security. Jack and Kyle struggled to appear unconcerned as they made their exit, but there was an air of suppressed excitement sparkling in their eyes.

Peter followed him upstairs and hovered behind as Archer unlocked his door. 'I – um – don't suppose I could have a close look at that bow could I? Now you've told me about making it yourself I'm quite curious.'

'Sure. Give me a couple of minutes to set it up.' He went in and shut the door then quickly retrieved the quiver, taking out all but three of the training arrows. Inspecting the rounded wooden tip, he compared them to the lethal metal barbs. They would still hurt if they were fired at a person, but they would not do as much damage as those designed to kill. Retrieving the bow, he strung it deftly – there was no point risking it being broken in their attempts to force the string over the nocks.

Peter's interest and enthusiasm were genuine as he asked intelligent questions about the method and tools involved. He appreciated the feel of it, running his hands along the arms, seeming to get the same pleasure that Archer did from the smooth contours of the wood. After a close examination of the arrows, there was nothing more to say about the manufacture and Archer started packing the arrows back. He wasn't sure if he was ready to volunteer himself into the trap by suggesting that they went outside with the bow. Peter might get suspicious if he made it too easy, but if that was his intention, he was leaving it late.

'I don't suppose you would be able to show me how to use it? Properly I mean. I've had a go with toy bows where the arrows had little rubber suckers on the end, but I think this would be a lot harder.'

'I could show you, but you wouldn't be able to do much yourself. It takes years of practise on smaller bows to build up the strength to pull it back fully.' He demonstrated the correct technique of standing, holding the bow, slotting the arrow into the string and positioning one finger above the arrow's nock and two below. 'So now I would draw the bowstring back until it reached my ear, but I cannot do that in the house.'

'Couldn't you just show me and then let it go again without releasing the arrow?'

'No, you must never release the string like that without firing the arrow, there is nowhere for the stored energy to go and it could damage the bow.'

Peter looked at the floor, disappointment evident on his face and Archer sensed some kind of internal debate going on. He could guess the problem, Peter was basically a good guy and wouldn't want any part of the tussle that would follow if he tricked Archer into going outside with the bow. Well he needed to decide whose side he was on and make his stand.

He seemed to make the right choice. 'Oh well, thanks very much, I've learnt a lot. I suppose you've got studying to do now, so I'll leave you to it.'

He had almost reached the door when Archer decided he could afford to give him a chance. 'Actually I was thinking of setting up some kind of butt in the garden to practice with. You could give me a hand.'

'A butt? Like for water?'

'No it's a target made of earth so that the arrows do not get damaged when you fire them.'

'I could get some paper and draw circles on it. That would be awesome.'

'Oh we couldn't do it today. I haven't asked permission from your parents. I'm sure your Dad would not be happy about me messing around with piles of earth.'

'He'll be fine. There's some spare turf from when he had the patio laid …' Peter went into some detail about how they could organise it so that Dave wouldn't even know. Archer's eyes narrowed, they had obviously discussed this aspect of their wicked plot already, but he went along with it and ten minutes later they had a passable butt. While Peter was marking out thirty paces, Archer warmed up the bow, rubbing the arms with a soft cloth and gently stretching the string, carefully controlling the return. Peter had marked rings on the paper with a thick black pen using a teacup, a small plate, a dinner plate and a rubbish bin. They weren't the normal diameters but at this distance it would suffice.

'You must stand behind the line and watch what I do.' Although it had been several weeks since he had practised, the years of training meant that his actions were smooth and fluid as the three tips pierced the central circle with almost no space between them.

Peter was clapping excitedly. 'Wow, that was amazing. Three bulls eyes. And so fast, your hands were a blur.'

As they retrieved the arrows, Archer heard a door shutting in the house, but he ignored it, asking Peter if he wanted to have a go.

'Could I? But I thought you said it takes years to build up the muscles.'

'If you tried from fifteen paces, you may be able to do it. You don't need to draw the string back so far.' As he marked out the distance and set his quiver down as the toe line, Archer caught a movement out of the corner of his eye. He was fairly sure they would wait until Peter had shot all three arrows so that there were as far away from Archer and the bow as they could be.

Peter had remembered a surprising amount from his brief description and demonstration, all Archer had to do was tilt the bow a few degrees so that the arrow could rest in the V formed by the handgrip and Peter's hand. He turned the arrow so that the white cock feather was turned out perpendicular to the bow.

'Where do I aim?'

'Just above where you want it to go.' His first arrow went to the left of the paper, so he adjusted slightly and the second one went into the paper on the right of the target and a little high. The third one was inside the outer circle and Peter was pleased, punching the air with a fist. As Archer went up to retrieve the arrows, it happened, just as he had predicted.

Fourteen

'You think you're so cool, just because you can fire a few arrows. Well anyone can do that. Just watch.' Jack held his hand out for the bow.

Peter didn't hand it over straight away. 'It's not as easy as it looks. You should have a go on the butt first.'

'Listen to mister know-it-all. Just because he's told you a few of the technical terms doesn't make you an expert.'

'I'm not saying I'm an expert. Just that any sportsman has to do warm up exercises before they go for it.'

'Maybe you should all have a go and whoever gets closest to the bull can try for the apple.' Archer was extremely calm considering the potential danger he was in.

'No-one asked your opinion, freak. Just shut up.' Kyle was brave when Archer was fully restrained, but his fear of tackling the warrior was obvious by the smell of nervous sweat surrounding him.

It had gone pretty much as Archer imagined it would. Before he could reach the butt, two bodies had come hurtling out from behind the thick hedge that screened off the rubbish dump from the rest of the garden. Once a compost heap, it was now piled high with the remains of rusted bicycles and tatty old garden furniture and toys. Archer knew they were there but feigned surprise at their attack, allowing the two of them to restrain him once more with the bungee with the minimum of resistance. Just a token punch or two and a good stamp on Jack's foot as he adjusted the cords on the front of his body.

Peter seemed to be as surprised as he was. He didn't actually help with the capture, but didn't do anything to prevent it either, merely retrieving the quiver and arrows, then watching without comment as Jack punched his captive in the stomach in return for the throbbing foot. So far it was actually working out better than Archer dared hope, Peter's slight resistance to Jack's superiority could be the start of his return to being the half-decent human being Archer was sure lay beneath the nastiness.

But it was not to be. Peter was too used to being dominated by Jack and too afraid of the consequences. Archer watched with a sinking heart as Jack checked to make sure Kyle was just behind his shoulder, then squared up to Peter, seeming to grow several inches taller as he held out his hand for the bow. 'I'm not going to ask you again. Give me the bow or I'll use it to tear you a new hole.'

Peter looked uncertainly in Archer's direction, then dropped his head slightly as he unslung the bow from where it had been resting on his shoulder, looking defeated as he held it out to Jack.

With a triumphant 'Ha,' Jack reached out, only to be thwarted as Peter snatched it back at the last instant.

'Who put you in charge anyway? I bet you couldn't even fire an arrow, let alone hit the target. I say the one who shoots closest to the bull, gets to do it. You'd like a go Kyle, wouldn't you? It's not fair that Jack always gets to have all the fun while we just have to watch.'

'It can't be that hard, we watched you doing it. Yeah, I'd like a go.'

Archer watched in amazement as Peter took control, pacing out the fifteen yards and placing the quiver there. Jack was no fool, he knew that he would learn more by watching the others' mistakes, so he let Kyle go first. The arrow just did a nose dive, so Peter made a couple of corrections, showing him how to slot the bowstring into the nock and straightening his left arm. Kyle's second arrow passed close to the target and the third was just inside the outer ring. Peter casually picked up the first arrow and straightened one of the feathers. 'I think he should get another go with this, it was a mistake.'

'If you think it will do any good, go ahead.' Jack still must have thought he was going to do better.

Kyle's last arrow was a little closer to the centre, but still outside the second circle. Peter insisted on putting a K next to the hole in the paper, in case of disputes.

Jack's short attention span was kicking in and he insisted on going next. His first arrow went way low, glancing off the side of the plastic bin, so he aimed higher the next time and it went way above the target. 'This is rubbish. I'm going to do those two again.' He went and picked them up, kicking the quiver a foot or so closer as he did. No-one commented, Jack was showing himself up so badly they didn't need to say anything to humiliate him further. He took a little more care with the third arrow and it actually clipped the edge of the paper.

Archer could see that Peter was thinking about offering some advice, but he closed his mouth without saying a word and grinned, covering his mouth with his hand as though he was going to sneeze or cough. The next arrow was just outside the outer ring and his last one was just inside it.

Peter marked it with a J, then collected the three arrows. He stood behind the quiver, taking his time to settle down and position his feet as Archer had shown him. He nocked the first arrow with the cockfeather on the inside, but it still found the second ring. The second shaft went inside the third ring and Kyle looked impressed.

'Well that's not fair, he's had more practise than us.' Jack was determined not to lose.

Peter put his arm down. 'That was my fifth arrow and it did better than your fifth arrow, so I've won anyway.'

'How do we know you didn't do more before we got here? You could have had loads of goes.'

'For God's sake Jack, stop being a sore loser. He's beaten you fair and square. If he says that was his fifth arrow, I believe him.' Kyle's face showed disgust tinged with fear, it was probably the first time he had dared to cross Jack.

'It's not about what you believe. I'm in charge here and I say we can't count Peter's last arrow.'

'Yeah, but even his fourth one was much closer than your fifth one. Face it Jack, you've lost.' As Kyle spoke, Jack made a grab for the bow, but Peter must have guessed what was coming and raised the arrow level with Jack's head, slowly drawing back the string.

'No Pete, stop.' Archer's shout had no effect; Peter had that same crazed look on his face as when they were racing back to the farm.

'Do you know what Jack? I'm sick of you bullying everyone. Just because you're bigger and stronger than other kids, you think you can make their lives a misery. I know you had it rough, but I've had enough of you turning my home into a battleground.' He took a breath and continued, keeping the arrow pointed at Jack's head all the time. 'Archer's ten times the boy you'll ever be and he's never so much as lifted a finger against you even though he could beat you to a pulp if he wanted to. He's trained in all sorts of fighting, but does he use it to pick on people weaker than him? No. He's kind and thoughtful and everything you'll never be.'

'Including a master of escape.' Archer had freed himself while Peter ranted and was right behind him. 'Thanks for the compliments Pete, but if you let that go it would do some serious damage and you'd be in proper trouble with your folks. Just lower your left arm and slowly release the tension in your right arm.'

Peter looked at him and blinked as though something released within him. 'Archer. I didn't know anything about this, honestly.'

'I know. Please Pete, it's not good for the bow to be under tension for that long.'

'What? Oh, yes.' He released it as Archer had instructed. Jack started to sidle off.

'Just a minute, where do you think you're going?'

'Upstairs. I can't be bothered with this poncey stuff.'

'You only call it poncey because you couldn't do it. With proper instruction I'm sure you can get all three in the bull in no time.'

'Would you show us Archer? That would be well cool.'

'Sure Kyle. But Pete still has one shaft to fire. I think you might do it this time, but first I should tell you a bit more about aiming. We didn't get that far.'

After the briefest of tuition on how to aim, Peter's sixth arrow landed on the thick black line of the inner circle - a bullseye. They spent another hour in the garden with Archer as tutor and by the end of it all three boys were getting all three arrows within the second circle. Jack even managed to get one in the bull, and he high-fived everyone with both hands.

That day marked a complete shift in every aspect of Archer's life and changed every member of the household. Julie couldn't believe the difference, she never had to wash up after a meal again and despite the fact that it was the summer holidays, she would often find the four of them studying hard. Archer had a good grasp of the complex mathematics involved in many sporting activities and was able to teach them things about angles and measures that none of the teachers at school ever could. In return, they brought him up-to-date with many differences in the language, giving him a broad exposure to the many slang expressions he might be likely to encounter. Kyle had a talent for English and drama that the other two weren't aware of and he was able to help in the study of poems and stories. The very best thing was that Dave was so impressed with the change in them, he replaced the broken monitor. So began Archer's biggest love affair – with computers.

Fifteen

'Come on Archer, let me have a go, you've been on there for two hours.'

'Eighty minutes. I still have ten to go.'

'What are you doing anyway? It's not a game.'

'Why would I waste my time playing something to test my reflexes or knowledge of strategy, when I can do it for real? If you want to play games, go on the Game Boy or the Mega Drive.'

'Peter's on one and Kyle's on the other.'

'Jack. Come back in ten minutes. If you ask me one more question I shall make it fifteen.'

Archer clicked a button and the page of strange looking text turned into a familiar internet page, but with boxes splitting the page up into sections.

'Oh my God. You've made your own internet page. There's Pete and me an' Kyle. How did you do that?'

'Hang on one minute.' He switched back to the source, changed a one to a zero, then clicked again and all the boxes disappeared, but the pictures stayed where they were. 'That's useful. You can switch the border on or off. Neat. Ok, all yours.'

'But how did you do that? Where did you get those pictures?'

'Julie had them on the computer, she said I could use them.'

'Can you make me a page? Is it hard?'

'You have to use a smart language called HTML. It's quite straightforward once you know what the rules are.'

'Blooty hill Archer, is there anything you can't do?'

'I don't think so. There's lots of things I haven't done yet, but I'm fairly sure I could if I wanted to.'

'Smug get.'

'Not really. Confident maybe, but what's the point in being any other way? If you go in thinking you can't do something, you've lost before you start. Better to believe you can. I'm not saying I could do everything well, but at least I could have a dashed good go at it first.'

'Here endeth the lesson for today.'

'Ballcocks.' Jack grinned at Archer's extended emphasis of the word. They had delighted in teaching him several swear words, hoping he would use them in front of Dave or Julie. After getting caught out once, he was wise to them, asking for an explanation for each new word. If he was in doubt, he would ask Julie if he had understood the word correctly at meal times. After the second time this happened, Dave got quite angry about "that kind of language" being used in his house. They gave it up as a bad job. Archer came up with the idea of using very similar sounding words when they felt the need to expel intense emotion and somehow only a swear word would do. Their repertoire extended to include such gems as "bells" or "walls", "muck" or "buck" and "plastard". Ballcocks was the firm favourite, it used two rude words and if challenged they could claim that they had just remembered what was needed to fix the toilet.

Unfortunately, the teachers at the school didn't seem to appreciate the joke and Archer was sent to the head for "inappropriate language" on his first day at the new school. The head was a stern-looking man with grey hair.

'So Mr Archer, a poor start. My first impression of you is not a good one. Inappropriate language indeed. I don't know what your last school was like, but we will not tolerate it here.' He glared at him over the top of his glasses as though expecting Archer to say something.

Archer wasn't sure what so he said nothing.

'Do you have nothing to say for yourself boy?'

'I was just trying to answer her question sir. The teacher asked us to give an example of something that was extremely likely and I said walking in cow shit on Glastonbury Tor. The tower's full of it you see ...'

'That's quite enough. Who was your teacher?'

'Miss Lowry sir.'

'This was in a maths lesson?'

'Yes sir. She was telling us about probability and about eighty percent of the floor was ...'

'Alright, that's quite enough. What I was really expecting was an apology, not a string of excuses for your bad behaviour.'

'I'm sorry sir, I didn't realise telling the truth was poor behaviour.'

'How dare you? I shall be speaking to you parents ...'

'They're dead sir. At least my mother is. My father disappeared shortly after.' This was delivered in a voice devoid of emotion; Archer was just regurgitating facts, none of it meant anything to him. Instead of showing compassion however, it seemed to infuriate the man even more.

'Well somebody must be responsible for you. Where are your records? Well. That explains it. David and Julie Reid. Parents of Peter Reid and foster parents of Kyle French and Jack Minton.' He closed the file with a snap and sat back in his chair. 'Say no more. A bigger trio of scoundrels you'll never meet. I don't know what goes on in that household, but I can't imagine it's a very stable place to send an impressionable young boy. I think a call to social services is required. Off you go. Try to behave yourself for the rest of the day.'

Archer stood up and watched as the man started making notes on a piece of paper. He couldn't allow good people to get into trouble because of his ignorance. But if he said anything it might make matters worse. He looked at the man, trying to work out a strategy that would pierce his air of self-important intolerance. There didn't seem to be too many options open to him.

'Are you still here boy? I thought I told you to go.'

'You did sir, but I'm afraid that if you make that call to these social services there will be a grave injustice. Dave and Julie Reid are working very hard to provide a decent foster home for some very wilful boys.'

'I cannot believe what I'm ...'

'Please hear me out sir. I honestly did not mean to offend anyone with my language or manners. Things are different where I come from. But I don't think it fair that they should be punished for my ignorance.' Archer could see a slight unbending in the man's face and made his plea. 'Please give them a chance to show how they have mended their ways, just one week is all I ask. If you do not see an improvement then go ahead and make your call.'

There was a long minute of silence while the man looked at him and Archer held his gaze, hoping that he would be swayed by simple honesty and sincerity. But it was apparently the wrong thing to do. He added another word to the note: impertinent. 'I don't know what this world is coming to when sixteen-year-old boys think they can tell an experienced head teacher how to run his school. I believe I told you to go several minutes ago.'

Archer had no choice but to return to his class, but he made a point of seeking out the others at break.

'So I hear you had your first run in with old Bar-stard.'

'Not a bad day's work. You've beaten the record by a mile. Peter took a year, I was a month and we thought Jack was doing well at one week.'

'But you didn't even get through an hour, let alone a day. Way to go champ.' Jack held his hand for a high five, but Archer didn't meet it.

'I wasn't trying to be rude, I just though shit was your word for what we call dung.'

'I reckon that pays you back for your little tactic up on the Tor. I don't mind telling you, I was shit scared.' Peter clapped him on the back and the others demanded to know what he was talking about, so he told them. They were suitably impressed that Archer had climbed it so easily.

'Look guys, there is something you can do for me. Do you like staying at Dave and Julie's?'

'Yeah it's ok, why?'

'I've been in worse. Far worse.'

'Because if Mr Barston has his way, they won't be allowed to foster any more. He's ringing up social services to complain.'

'That's not fair. What have they done?'

'Well he's saying it's what they haven't done. Sorry Peter, but he's really got a problem with the three of you. Called you a trio of scoundrels.'

'What's that when it's at home?'

'Someone who behaves badly and causes trouble at school. Like you lot.'

'Yo bros.' They were so caught up with congratulating themselves that they didn't hear the bell go.

'Look, promise me you'll try to stay out of trouble until I can explain. Unless you'd prefer to be split up and sent off to other foster homes.' That finally got through to them and they were subdued as they went off to their classes.

When they got back together at lunch time, Archer explained how he'd asked the head to hold off the phone call for a week to assess their improved behaviour.

'What good will that do?'

'Because if he's saying Dave and Julie don't know how to bring you up properly and he's got a stack of yellow slips to back him up, they'll believe him.'

'But if we can act like goody-goodies for a few days then they won't have any yellow slips to back him up.'

'You could even get some blue slips.' Peter sounded doubtful.

'What are they for?'

'Good behaviour. I had quite a few in year seven.'

'Do they still give them out in year eleven?' Kyle looked like he didn't believe they would carry on with childish stuff like reward slips.

'If you ask for them. That's what Harry did in maths when he finished the work.'

'That's it then. We each try and get a blue slip every lesson 'til the end of the week.' Peter looked hopeful.

Archer was more realistic. 'Maybe just one a day. But you should try to keep it up for at least a month.'

'As if.' Jack snorted his derision.

'OK, if you want to be split up or sent back to young offenders ...'

'Alright.'

'Sorted.'

'Seal the deal guys.' Peter put up his hand and everyone high-fived it.

Sixteen

'Come on Archer, tell us what it's like in this new place, is it better than here?'

'Pretty much the same really.' He hated lying to Finn and Fletch, but Malduc had been completely strict on that point. Archer was only allowed to see his friends if he told them nothing about the differences in his new world.

'What about the people, are they very different?'

'Not much. They spend all their time taking the p... teasing each other just like you guys.'

'And they speak differently. You're using many new words and phrases. Like guys.'

'That means the same as folk.'

'What about the girls? Anyone as pretty as my Bethia?'

'I'm sure there is, but I can't say I've noticed. Tell me what's been going on. How do you like being seniors?'

'It's really hard work. No idling off in these classes. If you don't do the task in lesson time, you have to finish it by the next day and they give you extra work.'

'That sounds harsh. We ...'

'Archer.' His name was almost a squeal. 'They said you were back. Patricia, Kayleigh, come over here.'

Archer stood up and kissed Bethia's cheek and Kayleigh hugged him and then he stood before Patricia, neither of them knowing quite what to do.

'Kiss her you dullard.' Fletch was practically pushing them together and they both blushed as Patricia stumbled into his arms. He turned it into a hug, finishing with a shy kiss on her lips which brought applause.

The rest of the day went by too quickly for Archer, it was good to be back and it was almost as though the past ten weeks had never happened. Bethia and Fletch were still kissing and cuddling whenever they thought no-one was looking and a blush tinged Finn's cheek when Archer caught him holding hands with Kayleigh. His two friends still insulted and teased each other at every opportunity and Patricia was just as shy and lovely as ever. The circle of friends now included Tybalt and Chrisya, Logan and Dervla and Machin and Rhianna. Everyone had paired off except for Patricia and he hated the fact that he couldn't tell her that he wouldn't be back for several years.

Part of him knew it wasn't fair to ask her to wait for him, but a much bigger part wanted her to stay free so that they could share the time together when he was back. All Malduc would let him say was that it was a distant place and that he would only be coming back for a day every few months. There was so much he wanted to tell her about in his new life, but he was not allowed.

'So this woman you're living with, is she very young?'

'I have no idea. Julie's probably a bit older than your Mum … mother, it's hard to tell.'

'Is she pretty?'

'I don't know. You don't think of someone's mother as pretty. She's warm and caring and works far too hard.'

'Oh.' Patricia didn't look happy.

'When I first got there, all the boys used to treat her like a servant – even her husband Dave, but I used to help her in the kitchen. I didn't think it was fair that she should do all the work while they just sat around.'

'That was good of you.'

'Yeah, well they just take advantage. And she's really smart, she taught me so many things about … well about everything really. I wish I could describe how different it is over there, everything is just … faster.'

'It sounds fearsome.'

'It is a bit, but you get used to it.'

'What about the others. Are they all as smart as Julie?'

'Hardly. Dave works as some kind of craftsman, but she reads other people's books and corrects their mistakes. You have to be really clever …'

'Alright Archer, I understand you think this Julie woman is wonderful, but I wa …'

'Patricia, I do believe you're jealous.'

'I am not. How would you like it if I spent ten minutes describing how good Finn was on the back of a horse or how no-one could beat him in the joust …'

'No really? He'll be getting far too big for his boots.'

'… or how tall he's grown …'

'Maybe I should set up for a joust next time.'

'… or how well he fills out his new …'

'Patricia. Has Kayleigh heard you talking about her boyfriend like this?'

'What?' She blushed deeply. 'I was just using him as an example, I could have talked about Fletch or Tybalt.'

'I believe you. I'm not sure Finn would. Or Kayleigh. Ouch. What did you do that for?' He rubbed his arm where she hit it.

'Because you are being deliberately slow. I'm trying to say have you met any other girls?'

'Not really, there are several in my class but I don't even know their names yet. Anyway, why would I want to meet any other girls? They would only beat me.'

Patricia shook her head in exasperation. It was obvious that was as close as she would get to any kind of admission of his intent.

Archer spent several hours with Lynette, Malduc and Kalen going over his experiences. When he reached the part about the boys' treatment of him, Lynette was angry.

'This is not reasonable Malduc. How can you expect him to defend himself against this sort of cruelty when he cannot use his powers in the other world?' She turned on Archer. 'And why did you not call or leave a message? I gave you my 'phone number.'

'I did not know how to use the telephone then.'

'Yes that's true. Sorry Archer. I take so many of these things for granted. I forgot how much there would be to tell you about, we should have had more than two days. Especially when most of the time was wasted waiting to see people.'

'It's alright, really. I have picked things up quickly with Julie's help.' He went on to explain about his run-in with the head at the school and how he had threatened to call social services. He also explained the boys plan to thwart him.

'This is terrible. Dave and Julie will lose their licence over this and it will be our fault. We must do something.'

'It seems that Archer has put a good strategy into place. I'm sure it will all work out well.' Malduc smiled his encouragement.

'No you don't understand. The people in power over there are very different from our council. They don't listen to the evidence of the common men and women. They are too easily swayed by the opinions of these officials. Judgements are made according to laws that make no sense for any of the people involved. We need to get Archer away from them as soon as possible.'

'What about Penny and Todd?'

'I'll try again. They said they would do it if we couldn't find anywhere else, but ...'

'Kalen. Can you get a sense of this?'

'I will try. But it will be difficult because he has been away for so long.' Kalen put his hands on Archer's head and closed his eyes, concentrating for a minute or two.

'I am sorry, it is very faint. I sense many trials, but nothing about the outcome. All I can perceive is that whether he is successful or not, he will need to learn from the outcome of each trial. The lessons he will learn about himself are more important than whether he succeeds or fails. Every experience will help him to fulfil his destiny, but we cannot tell yet what that is.'

'Thank you Kalen. Wise words. Wise words indeed, I'm sure we can all benefit from their message.'

Archer had no idea what it meant, but it didn't sound like anything was going to be easy any time soon.

Seventeen

Looking at Lynette as she carefully negotiated the turns in the road, Archer suppressed his annoyance. She was the driving force behind his transfer from Dave and Julie's to this new place. He felt sick to his stomach at the thought of going through the process of meeting new people and settling down again and had tried to put his point of view across. 'I don't see why I couldn't have stayed with Dave and Julie, I was just starting to fit in.'

'I know, I'm really sorry, but it wouldn't have worked out there.'

'Why not? The boys were starting to change their attitude and accept me. They were really trying to behave well and offer some support to Julie.'

'I know that's a good thing, but I'm not sure they will keep it up for much longer. I'm worried that the head will send social services in. If they start poking around, I'm sure they'd find something irregular about your records.'

'You said they explained where I've been.'

'Yes, but it won't stand up to close scrutiny. And isn't it better that you move to a different school if that head is already gunning for you?'

'He has a gun?' Archer was fascinated by the weapon that replaced the bow as the most lethal killing instrument.

'It's just an expression. It means he is looking to make trouble for you.'

'I haven't made a good start, have I? Malduc said that I must keep my head below the parapet and I seem to have raised it so high that it has caused trouble for everyone.'

'Not at all. You mustn't beat yourself up over it. Oh dear, that means you mustn't blame yourself. We do use rather a lot of violent expressions in this world.'

'I like that one. You're saying I mustn't inflict the pain caused by thinking I was at fault.'

'Exactly. It is much more important that you learn from it, as Kalen said. So don't go trying to change the kids at this new place, just accept that they are different.'

'Alright.'

'And keep a low profile at this new school.'

'Is that the same as keeping my head down?'

'Yes. Try to blend in with the other kids and if you're not sure what a word means, ask the teacher privately, not in front of the whole class. Or use a dictionary, I'm sure Penny will have one she can lend you.'

'I bought one myself. I got fed up asking people what words meant and they were pissed off having to explain.'

Lynette pulled into the drive of a rather untidy looking semi and turned to him with a smile. 'I can see you have been learning a lot, but whereas fed up is perfectly acceptable, I'm afraid the other phrase is not.'

'I'll never get the hang of it. There's far too much to learn.'

'You'll be fine. You're already sounding more like one of them than one of us. The more you read and watch TV, the more quickly you will pick it up. There is just one more thing I have to ask.'

The look on her face suggested that she was not happy asking the question and that he would not be happy with her request. 'Ask it.'

'Your bow. You should not have it over here.'

'What? Malduc said it would be alright.'

'I know. That's because he doesn't know what it is like over here. From the TV shows he saw, he imagines that everyone goes around with weapons to defend themselves, but it's not like that.'

'But if I do not practise regularly, I will lose the skill.'

'I know about that, but after what happened with those boys it's too dangerous. They have no idea that it is a lethal weapon used for killing people, they just see it as a toy. Imagine what would have happened if you hadn't stopped Peter from firing at Jack.'

'But I did. And I have learnt from it, I promise. I would never let anyone use it but me.'

'I'm afraid that isn't good enough Archer. It's too unusual and enticing for the children in this world. We have designed a compromise. I will keep it at my house and you can come over whenever you want to practise.'

He wasn't happy, but he could see the sense of it.

The first thing that struck Archer about his new home was the smell. It was much more like the homes he was used to, with the honest aromas of beeswax and home baking, natural herbs and flowers. None of the artificial smells of little gadgets that filled the air with chemicals supposed to imitate spring meadows or pine forests.

The second was the warmth and love that seeped out of every sunshine filled corner. It was displayed on every wall and surface in a jumble of photos and certificates, paintings and little notes with uplifting messages. There were pictures of happy things like flowers, hearts and smiling faces. He couldn't imagine anywhere more different to Julie's perfectly ordered home, this was what Finn's Mum would have called "an absolute pigsty."

Penny herself was the embodiment of her home, plump, cheerful and messy, but with a face that could turn strict and scary as soon as her eyes stopped twinkling. Her first act was to smother him in a hug, her second to push a plate of freshly baked ginger and date muffins under his nose.

'Help yourself. Penny is the best cook in Wiltshire, possibly in the world.' Lynette picked the smallest one and bit through the top. Archer followed her example and a big smile lit up his face. This was more like the food he was used to, cakes in Julie's house came out of packets and were too sweet. She had apologised as his nose screwed up after his first bite, and he learnt that it was the artificial ingredients, in particular the E numbers that caused that effect.

'Mmmm, this is good,' he said, his mouth still full of the rich flavours which melted on his tongue like nectar.

'I'm sorry to love you and leave you, but I don't want to be late picking Rory up. You know my number, call me if there's any sort of problem, not that there will be.' She gave Archer a hug, then turned to Penny. 'I can't thank you enough for this, I know you were trying to run it down for a while, but this really is an emergency. I'll be back soon with some more stuff. I'm hoping to get him a bike so he can cycle over to see us.'

'I'm sure we can lend him one until then. Drive safely.'

Archer's new room was nothing like the one at Julie's. No two pieces of furniture matched, they were all different colours and styles and many had been lovingly repaired and restored. The one thing that seemed out of place was a dusty looking computer. She was watching for his reaction and he didn't disappoint her, running straight over and pressing a few keys and moving the mouse. Nothing happened and he turned round with a question on his face.

'It's not plugged in yet, it needs three sockets. Todd said he'd bring an extension board home tonight. Don't get your hopes up too high, it's a very old model, doesn't play all the fancy games you boys seem to love.'

'Will it have the internet?'

'Yes, I think so.

'Then it will be perfect. I can use it to help me explore the planet. How many other people will need to use it?'

'Just you. Tom can use the one in the study if he needs to look things up, but he's happy with his Nintendo thingy for games and the girls don't care for it.'

'Thank you very much. I could help out round the house to help pay you back for your kindness.'

'Oh you will get your list of chores just like everyone else, but I won't be expecting too much, I know you will have a lot of studying to do for your exams. Julie told me you like to read as well; I'll show you the library when you come down, but I expect you'd like a little while to settle in first.' She looked down at his small bag with a smile. 'About ten minutes?'

'Try two. I travel light.'

'Well the bathroom is just along the hall if you need it.'

He was examining her collection of ancient myths and legends when the noise level went up by several hundred decibels. Tom, the only foster boy staying there had arrived home with a couple of his friends and Archer could hear Penny trying to persuade the other two boys to wait outside while she introduced Tom to the new guest.

'Don, I'd like you to meet Tom.' It took Archer a minute or two to realise that she was talking to him, Don was the name they had chosen for him over here, but at Julie's, everyone had been happy to call him Archer. He turned round and held his hand out but Tom just stared at him as though he recognised him.

'Oh my God, it's Robin Hood.' He ran out.

Eighteen

Everything about this place was different to Archer's previous two foster homes, it was a testament to Penny's diverse, esoteric interests. So you might find a glitter-enhanced painting of twilight turning a copse into a fairy grotto next to an old and battered plastic badge with the adage "Make love, not war" resting on a shelf next to a broken corn dolly, a statue of Buddha and an exquisitely crafted silver bell, which tinkled magically when shaken.

Archer's favourite objects were the natural ones, unusually shaped stones or sea shells and pieces of bark and gnarled twigs, even branches. Some of these were carved or polished to bring out their beauty, others lay as they would have in their normal environment, any cracks or crevices still housing earth, moss or lichen. It was obvious that Penny felt the same connection to earthly objects that his people did. For the first time since he had entered this different world, Archer began to feel at peace.

It was not destined to last long however, "the girls" Penny had spoken of were sisters Mandy and Kellie who were caught up in a messy divorce. They spent most of their time at Penny's, but stayed with their grandparents occasionally and would continue to do so until the courts decided the final outcome. This upheaval meant that their behaviour was extreme and usually obnoxious, hence their placement with Penny who was known to run a tight ship.

Sixteen-year-old Mandy had shaved all her hair off apart from a central stripe which was dyed bright pink and gelled into stiff peaks in the Mohican style. He was intrigued by the ugliness, finding out from the internet that it was a hairstyle favoured by a tribe of warriors living in America several centuries earlier. It also explained why her face was obscured with the matching war paint. Kellie was two years younger and dressed completely in black, with messy black hair and a white face in the Goth style. Archer didn't have a clue how to deal with them, they were like nothing he had ever met before.

'Watcha lookin' at gorgeous?' Mandy's first words caught him at a disadvantage because he had been staring.

'I'm not sure, the label's fallen off.' He used a phrase from an old TV show that made him laugh.

'Aw Gawd Kell, we've got us a right comedian here, pretty tasty one though.' She spanned his upper arm with her hands. 'Feel the muscle on that. You must work out every day.'

'I do work every day at school and in the house, but the muscle comes from ...' he hesitated, he was about to say from practising with the bow, but after the last load of trouble it was probably better not to mention it.

'Gor blimey, listen to Mr Posh Pants. Mummy and Daddy send you to public school did they?'

He was baffled by their behaviour and said the first thing that came into his head. 'My real parents are dead.'

'Ain't you the lucky one? I wish mine were. Stupid prats haven't got a clue about anything and they spend all their time knocking seven bells out of each other and us.'

Archer was horrified. He had no idea what to say to her bleak statement or how to handle this pair of Valkyries as they circled him like prey, poking and prodding.

'Girls, leave the poor boy alone, I thought I told you to go up and put your stuff away and get on with your homework. I'll be coming up to check in half an hour.'

''Ow come 'ee doesn't 'ave to do 'is homework? Oh don't tell me, finished it already. Mr Goody Two Shoes.'

As they left, Penny smiled fondly. 'Take no notice of those two, their bark is much worse than their bite.'

'Was it true, that their parents beat them?'

Sighing, she rolled her eyes. 'I would take most of what they say with a pinch of salt, they don't seem to know the difference between fact and fiction. But deep down there are nice girls trying to get out from under all that make-up and bravado.'

Archer sighed, it was just like at Dave and Julie's, he was going to have to prove himself all over again. Not with Tom, he spent most of his time out of school either in his room playing some kind of computer game, or in the den at the bottom of the garden with his friends, a couple of rogues called Jason and Matthew. Maybe he would be lucky and the girls would spend all their time in their room doing girl things or even school work.

But that was just wishful thinking. Mandy seemed to take it as a personal challenge to make every encounter an opportunity to irritate Archer in some way. Her biggest weapon was the fact that she was a girl. His sense of honour was so ingrained that no matter how hard she tried to destroy his equilibrium or pierce his mantle of good manners, he denied her the reaction she craved. It started small, with her refusal to address him by his given name.

'Hey muscles, pass the spuds.'

Tom went to reach for the potatoes, he was smart enough to recognise the battle lines and his loyalties lay firmly with Archer.

'Leave it pipsqueak. I didn't mean you and you know it.'

'Maybe if you addressed people by their given names, they would understand your intentions,' Penny observed.

'They knew exactly who I meant. He's the pipsqueak 'cos he's small and he squeaks, and he's muscles 'cos he's a hunk who's built like a brick …'

'That's quite enough of that, young lady. You know I won't tolerate bad language in my house. It's a lack of vocabulary that gives you a sewer mouth.'

'If you think my mouth is dirty, you should …'

'Mandy. Here are the potatoes you asked for.' Archer's tone and look suggested that no-one was impressed and the only person she was letting down was herself.

'Why thank you Sir Galahad. Or is it Sir Lancelot?'

'Actually it's neither. He's Robin Hood.' Tom made the assertion for the second time and everyone looked at him in surprise.

'Ok, I give in, what makes you say he's some divvy who robs people and then gives it all away like a prat?'

Tom shrugged. 'He just is, that's all.'

'If you say so. Robin, can you pass the pepper please.'

So that was it. Ever after, she called him Robin but he refused to rise to it, even when she shouted it across the playground one day at school.

'Why's that Mandy calling you Robin?' Kevin, one of the boys he'd met on the first day at the school asked.

'No idea. Maybe she thinks I'm somebody else.'

She came up then with a couple of friends who also wore punk hairstyles. 'Oi, you. I was shouting you.'

'I'm sorry, my name's not Robin. I thought you meant someone else.'

'Very funny. Tell the witch that we won't be coming home tonight, we're going to my nan's.'

'Sorry, can't help you. Don't know any witches.'

She came up and grabbed hold of his shirt. 'Don't get smart with me. You're not big enough or hard enough.'

He took her hand and uncurled her fingers, releasing his shirt. 'I don't need to be big or hard to get smart with you. I just need to have opened a book once.'

'Why you cheeky little …' Her insult was cut off as the deputy head appeared telling them to get registration.

Archer thought she probably would have given any other teacher a rude retort as her friends dragged her off towards the English block. He followed Kevin and Jamie, who said under his breath, 'You've got a nerve, she's a right nutcase that one. And her sister.'

'Hard as nails they are, the pair of them. Not a good idea to wind her up like that if you want to live.'

'Oh I think I'll live. Just got to keep one step ahead of them.' Which was easier said than done. He knew where he was with Edlyn, his first real enemy, it was a case of when he was within ten yards, there would be trouble. Similarly with Jack, Kyle and Peter, he knew that he needed to be on guard constantly, looking for traps round every corner. But it was different with the girls, quite apart from his reluctance to engage in conflict with the "fairer sex" as Sedge would call them, there were the constant confusing signals they were sending out, particularly Mandy. For every remark that was intended to intimidate or ridicule him, there would be an accompanying look or gesture suggesting that what she really wanted was his support or approval, or even friendship. Beneath her war paint and aggressive manner he sensed a loneliness and vulnerability, borne from many years of standing up for herself and her sister against a violent, hostile world.

And so he made his first mistake, feeling sorry for her; it was a mistake that would cost him dearly.

Nineteen

After a week or so, Archer seemed to be fitting in well and managing to keep away from trouble. By spending most of the time in his room, he avoided the girls and made a real impact on his school subjects. Although he had an aptitude for the maths related to real life problems and solid shapes and angles, he was struggling to grasp many of the more abstract concepts like prime factors and linear equations. He had never used any of the basic computer packages like word processors and spreadsheets, but once Tom had spent a couple of evenings showing him the tricks, he was able to use the online help to teach himself. There were still lots of gaps in his knowledge, but he became quite proficient at using the search engines to interrogate the internet about pretty much anything.

On the day he met Rory for the second time, because of the name, Archer was expecting a boy. Penny had asked him to find out what was taking so long and the scream had him running toward the danger.

'What's going on? Rory? Are you alright?' He ran towards the sound of the voice and was nearly knocked over for the second time in ten minutes. He held out his hands to steady the small figure and was rewarded with kicks and scratches as the little bundle of energy fought to escape. He let go immediately. 'You must be Rory.'

'Who are you?'

Archer had read about the "fight or flight" response and if ever there was a body poised to do that it was the one in front of him; he was obviously from warrior stock. It probably didn't help that Archer was towering above him by a couple of feet, adding to the threat. He sat down on the grass. 'Penny sent me, she was worried when you didn't come back straightaway.'

'What's your name?'

'Don Archer. I'm staying here for a while. Did those boys hurt you?'

'No.' The shake of the head revealed long hair, braided like a Viking. But not normally worn by boys in this century. Unless... he looked harder, obviously causing some distress as the little figure sat down. 'So you were just screaming because...'

'It was a game.'

'Which is why they ran off as soon as they heard me. All part of the game I suppose.' He was ninety nine per cent certain and the distinctly feminine shrug gave the last per cent. The brave little warrior was a girl.

'I – I,' Before she could finish, Tom appeared, demanding to know where Matt and Jason were.

'That's what I'm trying to find out. I think they were bullying our little guest here, but she's much too brave to snitch on them.'

Tom sat down next to them with a shrug. 'S'pose they can be a bit rough. Are you ok?' She nodded. 'Well I'll tell 'em you wouldn't rat an' make sure they leave you alone in future.'

As Tom made all sorts of promises he probably wouldn't be able to keep, Archer's stomach reminded him that it would need more food very soon and he suggested they got back. As he helped Rory up, she asked if he wasn't a bit old to be a foster kid, making Tom gasp at the word nobody seemed to want to mention. Archer tried to explain that this was just a place for him to study for a while, then they ran back down the garden.

Later that evening he tried to find out from Rory exactly what had gone on in the den that day, but she refused to tell, giving him a look that said he shouldn't ask again. Her pose suggested she was more than capable of standing up for herself against two older lads and his heart sank. He really didn't need another pushy female. *Were there no ordinary girls over here?*

First impressions however, can be deceptive. Despite her reluctance to discuss anything that had gone on that day, Rory turned out to be nothing like the tough little tomboy she was pretending to be. Being quite bright, she was the perfect person to fill in some of the gaps in his education. He learnt quickly under her patient teaching.

'So a square number is one that can be arranged into a square and a triangle number into a triangle.'

'It's obvious if you draw the dot patterns.'

'And if you can make a rectangle with the dots then it must be a multiple of the numbers. Like three rows of five gives you fifteen.' He finished the pattern with a flourish.

'Yes, and three and five are called the factors.'

'Got it. So two and eight would be factors of sixteen.'

'That's right.'

'And a prime number is,' he read from the book, 'a number that has no other factors except one and itself.'

'Like thirteen.'

'Or seven, or seventeen.'

'What's this Archer, are you teaching maths to Goldilocks?' Mandy picked up one of the books.

'Yes, but we'll have to finish now you're here.' Rory grabbed the book back and started packing away. Archer was surprised that Rory lied, but he could tell that she didn't like the older girl.

'Oh don't finish on my account. I don't get any of it and never will. I just came in to watch some TV.' She sprawled on the sofa with one leg resting over the side so that her short skirt was pulled down revealing the top of her fishnet stocking. 'Oops.' Just in case Archer's eyes weren't glued to her legs, she made a big deal of adjusting the skirt. Rory somehow managed to knock all the books onto the floor and he tore his eyes away to help her, jumping as the TV came on at full volume.

'Oops again. Sor-ry. Don't mind me.'

It took a while before he spotted that there was a pattern to this. Rory only came over once a week and if she spent any time with Archer, Mandy would find some excuse to interrupt whatever they were doing. If Rory sat on her own, or on the rare occasions she played outside with Tom or was in the garden with Todd, there was no sign of the scheming punk. Sometimes Archer would help with Rory's homework, but mostly they explored algebra and soon moved past the level she was working to at school. They were using Tom's maths book as Archer's was too advanced and it was a joint challenge to unpick the mysteries of number patterns and sequences. But they never managed more than half an hour before Mandy appeared, more often than not wearing something tight and revealing. When she interrupted, Rory picked up the books and they continued outside for a little while. Archer was baffled. 'What is wrong with that girl? Why can't she leave us alone?'

'If I didn't know better I'd think she was jealous.'

'Of doing maths. I hardly think so.'

'Of the fact that you're spending so much time with another girl.' Archer laughed and Rory looked quite hurt, turning away. He touched her arm. 'Hey munchkin, don't take offence, I didn't mean anything by it. But you're all of what, ten?'

'Nearly thirteen.'

'Twelve years old, and she's a big ugly old thing of sixteen.'

'Do you really think she's ugly?'

'It's just a saying. All that rubbish she puts on her face is ugly; I'm sure if she didn't wear it, she could be quite pretty. If she smiled more instead of snarling and stopped chewing that awful gum. It reminds me of a cow, chewing the cud.'

'Do you realise you just called her a fat ugly old cow?'

'I never called her fat.'

'You said big, that's the same.'

'Well I didn't mean it. She's got a nice body, but she's always showing it off. I don't like that.'

'I'm never going to wear make-up or chew gum.'

'You don't need to, you're pretty enough without it.' He touched the end of her nose and she blushed pink as she picked up a pencil to draw the next pattern.

The next week they were given some tricky equations for homework which had to be finished by the next day. The teacher said they were so easy she wasn't even going to bother explaining how to work them out. Archer knew Rory was coming that day, so he rushed home early to get there just as she arrived with Penny.

'Archer, I'm glad you're home early, I didn't get a chance to get to the post office today and it will be closed in half an hour. Would you mind looking after Rory while I pop out again?'

'No problem. We'll do some homework.'

'Good. Lynette says she's doing well with your help.'

Archer was pleased, it couldn't have worked out better, they might get it done before the others got back. As Penny left, he turned to Rory. 'Would you mind helping me with some maths? I've got quite a lot and it's really tricky.'

'Sure, no problem.'

'Hang on then, I'll just get the book.' He ran up to his room, and had to tip everything out of his backpack before spotting the worksheet. He turned round and nearly walked into her; she'd got bored with the wait.

'Sorry, couldn't find it. Come on then.'

'I like your room. It's cool.'

'Thanks. It's a bit of a mess. Have you done equations before?'

'Show me.' He handed her the worksheet and she sat down on the bed. 'Five x equals twenty. Well that's easy, five lots of four is twenty so x must be four.'

He sat next to her. 'So you multiply the number by the letter. Right. Let me do the next one. Six add y is twelve so y must be two.'

'No that's not right, you need to add this time, y is six.'

'Oh dear, I thought I'd got it.'

The first exercise was fairly straightforward and once he got the hang of it, they whizzed through them, but the next section had two steps. They managed the first four by trying lots of guesses for the answer until one worked, but question five was tough.

'Four x add five equals twenty three. x must be about four then.'

'No it can't be. Sixteen add five is twenty-one. It must be five.

'No, twenty add five is twenty five.'

'So it must be somewhere in the middle.'

'What the hell is going on here? Does Penny know you two are making out on Archer's bed?'

Twenty

Blushing, they jumped up and the books slid to the floor.

'Hey, Tom, Kellie, come and see this, they've been at it in Archer's room.' Mandy's tone was ecstatic.

'No we haven't, don't be silly.' Archer tried to calm down the situation, but Rory had a different idea.

'So what if we were? You're only jealous because you wish it was you.'

Tom and Kellie came in just in time to hear this and the evidence was damning. Archer and Rory were standing red-faced and there was a big dent in the quilt where they had been sitting.

'Look this is ridiculous, Rory was helping me with my maths homework.' Archer held out the worksheet.

'Aw come on mate, listen to yourself. A twelve-year-old is gonna be helping with GCSE maths? I don't think anybody would believe that. You must think we're really dumb.' Tom turned away and Mandy sneaked a victorious grin as she backed off to watch the fun.

Archer grabbed his arm. 'Honestly Tom, it's algebra, I've never done it before. Ask her any of the questions off the sheet, she can do them.'

'I looked up to you, but I don't like being lied to.' He shook Archer's arm off and stalked out.

'Honestly Kellie, I wouldn't be doing anything else, she is only twelve, you must believe me.'

'I think I'd rather believe her.' She pointed at Rory who had gone from bright red to deathly pale at his words.

'Rory, tell them the truth, we weren't doing anything. You didn't know what you were saying.'

Rory gave a great sob and ran out of the room. He went to run after her but Mandy stood in his way. 'I think you've done enough. Kellie, go and find her and make sure she's alright.' Kellie left and Mandy shut the door behind her, looking at Archer thoughtfully.

He appealed to her with an outstretched arm. 'Come on Mandy, you must have seen when you came in, we were sitting on the edge of the bed doing homework.'

'That's not what I saw. Yes the two of you were on the bed, but when I came in you both jumped apart blushing. Even if she hadn't blurted it out in front of witnesses, why else would you both blush?' Despite her innocent air, something in her manner told him she knew exactly what they were doing, but had her own reasons for twisting it.

'You … you …' he was lost for words.

'Try fat, ugly, old cow. Isn't that what you called me? Behind my back of course, you haven't got the guts to say it to my face.'

'I didn't say that.'

'So now I'm a liar as well? I heard it with my own ears. Out of the bathroom window.'

'So you must have heard the rest of it then.'

'No, I ran out in tears. She was right, I did fancy you once, but not any more. Not after that. How could I fancy a cradle-snatcher like you?'

'I'm sorry you were hurt, it wasn't like it sounded. If you'll let me explain …'

'Oh I think you'll be sorry. And you've got some proper explaining to do. That's the end of it for you here. Penny won't stand for anything like that under her roof and Todd will probably beat you black and blue. As for Lynette …' She was obviously enjoying her moment of power, but even from the depths of despair, he could sense that there was something behind all this, she wanted something from him. His expression hardened.

'What?'

She stopped prowling and assumed a false innocence. 'I don't understand.'

'What do you want from me?'

'What I want is for you to suffer the way you've made me suffer. Parading your muscles around, watching me with those liquid brown eyes, giving me false hope …'

'I didn't.'

'… while all the time you've been laughing behind my back with that little brat and calling me foul names.'

'I haven't. I told you we've been …'

'Shut it.' She came up and closed his mouth with her hand. They heard Penny's cheery, "It's only me."

Mandy hissed in his ear. 'You won't know when I'm gonna tell, it could be any time. But you will do exactly what I tell you or it will be sooner rather than later.'

'But …'

'I said shut it. I'll tell the others not to say anything, that I might have been mistaken. You must keep away from Rory. If I see you huddled up anywhere with her, I'll tell straight away. You're going to do my chores and if anyone finds out you're helping me, I'll tell.'

'Is that it?'

'Until I can decide exactly what to do with you, yes.'

So began the worst time in Archer's life so far. She was relentless in her mental torment of him, it was far worse than the physical punishment Edlyn or Peter had ever dished out. Somehow, she seemed to have power over the others, the incident was never mentioned again by Tom or Kellie and he was fairly sure Rory couldn't have mentioned it or Penny would have said something at the very least. He couldn't know for sure because he dare not talk to her for fear of Mandy carrying out her threats.

Two days later she cornered him on the landing. 'I need a written confession from you so you can't wriggle out of it and pretend it never happened.'

'I didn't do anything wrong. I will not lie and I certainly will not commit a lie to paper.'

'If you don't do what I say, it will be the end for you. You'll end up in a youth offenders' centre and poor Rory will be dragged through all the courts and have to tell everyone that she was in your bedroom.' She paused as a door opened downstairs, but it closed again and she moved closer. 'Even if you weren't actually doing anything, that will be enough to make everyone think that she's a tart. Can you imagine what would happen to her at school if they found out?'

Mandy was enjoying herself. With her eyes sparkling and a sultry smile, Archer could see that she could actually be quite attractive if she wasn't so nasty. He shivered, was she some kind of enchantress, enticing him with her dark powers? Her voice took on a low, sexy tone as she circled round him, weaving her spells. 'I'll tell you what would happen. People would start to talk about her and call her names. Nasty people calling her nasty names.'

'Nasty people like you.'

She laughed wickedly. 'Oh yes. I'd make sure that the very nastiest people found out exactly what she did. Then she'd find out what it was like to have people calling you names and saying hurtful things about you.'

She held out the pen and paper and he looked at it bleakly while he assessed the alternatives. He had always been brought up to believe that honesty was the best policy, but he couldn't see how that would help in this case. Not for the first time in his life, he was damned if he did and damned if he didn't. But this time the stakes were so much higher. He needed more time to think through all the options, but the impatient tapping of her foot said that his time was up. There was no choice but to go along with it for now. Taking the paper, he sat at the desk.

She followed him, the triumph evident in her voice as she dictated, 'I Archer, being of sound mind, do solemnly declare …'

He ignored her and wrote his own simple statement. She bent over his shoulder and read aloud. '"Rory and I were in my room" – that wasn't what I said.'

'If you want a testimony from me it will be in my own words. I will not use your words or something you have heard on the TV.'

'You're in no position to negotiate. You will do as I say or suffer the consequences.'

'Right now I'm thinking it would be better to take my chances with Penny. I'm sure she will be able to work out the truth.'

'Be my guest.' She stood back and gestured down the stairs. He stood up and walked towards them. 'But it's not just about you is it? What will Rory say? You don't know for sure do you? She was quite happy to let me think that you two had been kissing and the others heard her say it.'

'I'm sure she would realise how serious it is and tell the truth.'

'Are you? Absolutely sure? Anyway, it doesn't matter what you were doing. Just the fact that the two of you were alone together in your bedroom would be all it would take for some people. Remember what I said? People can be sooo nasty.'

He knew he was beaten and paused, turning to face her. She resumed her reading aloud of his statement. 'Now where was I? Oh yes, "Rory and I were in my room. She was helping me with my maths homework." You have absolutely no pride do you? Admitting that a twelve-year-old girl was doing your homework. What a dummy.'

He could have wasted more breath explaining that they were learning together, but it just wasn't worth it, she wouldn't have listened.

'You haven't said anything about the fact that you were alone together or for how long. You need to add that and sign it. Don't put the date.'

'Why not? So you could use it in a couple of months even after I've done everything you wanted me to? I will not sign it without a date.'

'Whatever. Just do it, I'm getting bored now.'

He wrote that they were in the room alone for about twenty minutes then signed and dated it. She grabbed it and read the words carefully, then folded it up and put it into her shoulder bag.

The next thing she did was to try and hurt Rory as much as possible by forbidding Archer to have anything to do with her. Mandy made sure she was home as early as possible on the days Rory came so he would have no chance to speak to her alone and explain the situation. As if this wasn't bad enough, Mandy started hanging around asking him questions about his homework. Surprisingly, she could discuss quite a lot of it with him because she was actually quite bright and had covered most of the work already in previous years. A tiny part of him appreciated the support, even though he suspected it was doing her more good than him because it was fresh in his mind whereas she had forgotten most of it.

He was acutely aware of Rory's pain because he was suddenly ignoring her and Mandy had taken over as his study partner. Except that she was trying to be so much more than that. Whereas Rory would sit on a different chair or on the opposite side of the table, Mandy's style was to get as close to him as she possibly could, squeezing next to him on the edge of his chair or wrapping herself around him at the table to read over his shoulder. She was always touching his arm or fiddling with his hair and at the start, he flinched away from her.

After a week he'd had enough, but she wasn't so suffocating on the days Rory wasn't there, generally giving him a bit more space. One Wednesday Rory was sitting on the sofa reading her book when he got in. She didn't even look up as he dumped his bag as normal to hunt a snack. When he came back in the room, Mandy was there and she hugged him, kissing his cheek.

'Did you want to have another look at that poetry? I've got the study guide so it might help you to understand the weird language.'

He looked over at the sofa uncertainly and she followed his gaze. 'I'm sure Rory won't mind letting us have the sofa so we can sit together. This is important GCSE work.'

Rory looked up, obviously not pleased.

'Or we could go up to your room, it would be quieter there. Nobody would mind, we are going out after all.'

Rory picked up her book and fled into the kitchen.

Twenty One

'What's up sweetheart? You're not your usual sunny self.' Penny looked up as she stomped over to the counter.

'Nothing. I just need a bit of peace and quiet.' Rory helped herself to a ginger biscuit from the plate.

'Oh dear, those girls can be a bit noisy. You could always go up to your room.'

'I can't concentrate with Tom's game next door.'

'You're welcome to stay in here. I'll turn the radio off.'

'No it's alright, the music doesn't disturb me.'

'You curl up in the window seat, I'll turn it down a bit.'

Silence was the last thing she needed. If it wasn't raining she would have run down the garden or played on the trampoline to get rid of some of the anger that was building up inside her. It just wasn't fair, none of it. Mandy was the most evil creature in the universe and now she had found a way to make Rory's life a total misery. The words in front of her swam out of focus as she recalled the various clashes they'd had in the few months since Mandy and Kellie had arrived at Penny's.

~*~

The first time had been a complete misunderstanding, Penny forgot to tell her the girls had moved into the "granny flat". The huge attic space was converted into a comfortable living space with a big bedroom, lounge area, bathroom and a tiny kitchenette. It was always flooded with sunlight in the afternoon and was Rory's favourite place for curling up with a book when it was unoccupied.

'What the...? Who the hell are you and what do you think you're doing in our room? Come to steal our stuff?'

'Nah, it's Goldilocks, she's come to try all the beds to find the right one.' Kelly cackled at her joke.

'Well she's not having any of *my* porridge. Get out and take your stuff with you.'

~*~

Rory shivered as she remembered the terror of being woken from a doze to find two witches from the very worst fairy tale swearing and shouting at her. Mandy had pulled her up and shoved her down the stairs, throwing the book after her, creasing several pages as it hit the wall.

After that bad first encounter it seemed that Rory couldn't do anything right, no matter how hard she tried to make up for what was just a simple mistake. Mandy would take great delight in disturbing her attempts to do homework when she came in from school, turning on the TV at ridiculously high volume. Or she would "accidentally" knock a book or pen and wait for a complaint so she could make a sarcastic retort. Then there was her apparent clumsiness at mealtimes which she always managed to blame on Rory.

But the worst was when things went missing from Tom's room. He mentioned it at a meal and Mandy kept referring to Rory's one trip to the attic room as though she did it all the time, calling her Goldilocks and asking whose armchair she had broken lately. Rory knew one of them had taken her favourite hair slide but didn't dare to say anything when she saw Kellie wearing it. There was nobody that she could talk to and when Lynette tried to find out why she was always quiet on the way back from Penny's, she would just say that she was tired.

She felt so isolated. Tom had his own friends and the girls didn't seem to pick on him because he was a bit older and bigger. When Archer arrived it was like there was finally someone on her side. After rescuing her from Tom's friends, he represented a layer of protection against everyone who might harm her. She began to see him as her own personal knight in shining armour.

Mandy seemed to leave her alone, for some reason she wasn't willing to bully her in front of Archer. But Rory knew Mandy was jealous of the way he spent time with her and kept trying to disturb them to get his attention. It was quite obvious that she fancied him, Rory saw the way she watched him at meal times when she thought no-one was looking.

Well now she had got what she wanted, they were going out together and they were welcome to each other. He had not turned out to be the hero she thought he was, letting that creature slobber all over him every chance she got. He hadn't even bothered to speak to her since that dreadful day. She shuddered at the memory of the awful moment when Mandy had looked at her with victory gleaming in her eyes. Rory hadn't meant to say what she did, it just slipped out, the need to hurt was too strong.

A splash of water hit the pages of her reading book and she blinked to clear her eyes which had suddenly blurred completely.

'You couldn't lay the table for me, could you Rory, I'm a bit behind?'

'Sure, Aunt Penny.' She put her bookmark in the right page, hastily wiping away the tear from the book and the ones in her eyes. Penny looked over and saw the gesture.

'Is everything alright sweetheart?'

'Yeah, it was just a sad bit.'

'I don't remember sad bits at the start of The Lion, The Witch and The Wardrobe, but I'll take your word for it.'

As she set the knives and forks out, Rory wanted to ask Aunt Penny if Archer really was going out with Mandy, but she was too afraid that the answer would be yes. She watched them as they ate the evening meal, he didn't seem to pay her any more attention than anyone else in the room. Mandy was certainly going out of her way to be extra helpful, not just to him, but to everybody, passing round the food, pepper and salt, even getting up to get the tomato sauce and refill the water jug. When she finished eating, her hand disappeared and Rory noticed a slow blush creep up Archer's neck. She felt sick and looked away. At the end of the meal it was Kellie's turn to wash up and Archer's turn to dry, but Mandy started filling the bowl, she had obviously swapped so they could be together. As Rory brought in some cups from the other room, she walked in on the pair of them kissing. Putting the cups down quietly, she went up to her room and flung herself on the bed. It was true then.

Twenty Two

As Rory ran out of the kitchen, Mandy let go and Archer closed his eyes in despair. He didn't know why the opinion and friendship of a twelve-year-old girl should matter so much to him, but it did. He felt the same kindred spirit within Rory as he did with Penny, Julie and Dawn, but definitely strongest with Rory. It was as though she understood what was important in life, things like nature and helping people and learning things. She didn't care for all the electronic gadgetry like the others.

Thanks to Mandy's devious tricks Rory no longer looked at him as though he was worthy of her admiration. In fact, she could hardly bear to look at him at all. He was still cringing at the way Mandy had manipulated him into this position, forcing him deeper into her web of deception. He thought back to the earlier scene. Anyone else might have been satisfied with commandeering the sofa and forcing Rory out of the room, but it wasn't enough for the monster Mandy had become.

~*~

'Every time I touch you, you flinch away. Don't you like being touched, or don't you like me?'

Archer refused to talk to her about such personal things, picking up the study guide to start work.

Snatching it off him, she turned his face until he was looking directly into her eyes which flashed with anger. 'You can't bear to touch me, so that will be your ultimate punishment. When you have convinced that silly little girl that you are my boyfriend and you want nothing more to do with her, then I might consider ripping up your confession and letting the matter drop.'

Archer clenched his jaw. This would be a living hell. He was so repulsed by her evil nature that the thought of touching her made his skin crawl as though covered in a thousand writhing maggots. If he could just find the courage to go through with it, it might only be a couple of day's suffering. He would only have to do it when Rory was there, normally one day a week. Gritting his teeth, he nodded his agreement and the change was instant as her anger turned to triumph and her voice softened.

'She will have to believe that you genuinely prefer me, so you will have to put on a good show. I'm a very touchy-feely girlfriend, so you'll have to learn to stop flinching. I promise you will get plenty of practise.'

True to her word, throughout the meal, every time she passed him something she managed to make their fingers meet. Getting up from her chair, she brushed against him and rested her hand on his shoulder when she reached over to get the water jug. She had crossed a line, putting her hand on his thigh when she finished eating, but there was nothing he could do without causing a big fuss, so he tried to ignore it. She'd persuaded Kellie to swap her duty so they were clearing up together and she was full of her victory. 'That little geek couldn't keep her eyes off you, every time I touched you her face dropped a mile.'

'You must feel very proud of yourself taking on someone so much older and wiser than you are.'

'Very funny. She winds me up with all that holier-than-thou turning the other cheek she does. No matter how nasty I am to her she just seems to bounce back and keep trying to make friends. It's not normal.'

'So you're nasty to her because she's nice to you. That makes sense.'

'It does to me. I didn't stand a chance of breaking through her shiny-happy barrier until you came along. When she lied about making out with you I found a crack in her defences. Now I can break her completely.'

'So you knew she was lying all along. That we weren't doing anything wrong.'

'Of course I did. But it's too late now.'

Archer was going to say something about what a nasty piece of work she was, but they heard Penny asking Rory to take the cups through to the kitchen and Mandy turned round and wound her arms round his head whispering, 'This is your chance to make her believe it.' Then she pressed her lips to his as he heard the door open.

~*~

Friday brought with it bad news, Rory was to spend the next week at Penny's while Lynette went down to London on a training course. This meant that Archer's supposed relationship with Mandy would be on show all week, but something really strange happened on the Saturday. The girls went into town as normal, dressed in their outrageous costumes and he did not see them return.

When she came down for the evening meal, Mandy was not the same girl at all, everything had undergone a radical transformation. The pink Mohican was replaced by long golden curls and the extreme make-up had disappeared, it looked as though she wasn't wearing any at all. Her skirt swung down past her knees in a pretty floral fabric and the blouse was a soft gypsy style which modestly covered all the tattoo-covered flesh she normally liked to expose at her midriff and shoulders.

Archer stood up to help her into her seat and she actually blushed as she thanked him, meeting his eyes shyly from under lowered lashes.

'Why Mandy, how lovely you look. I always knew there was a pretty girl under all that muck. Doesn't she look lovely Todd?' Penny's comment somehow included Archer and he couldn't help but nod his agreement as Todd muttered something about hardly recognising her.

'Thank you Aunt Penny. I think it's all down to you really, you have made me so welcome here, all of you.' Just in case anyone was in any doubt that she was especially talking about Archer, she put her hand over his where it lay on the table. Normally he would have moved his immediately, but her touch was brief as she continued, 'I'm really sorry if I've been horrid to live with for the past few months, but you are all showing me that people do care about us, even if Mum and Dad don't.'

Although Kellie hadn't changed her appearance, she too seemed to be influenced by her sister's humble manner, adding her appreciation. They were accomplished actresses and Penny and Todd seemed completely taken in by their performances. Tom didn't pay much attention apart from a comment that she "cleaned up pretty well" but Archer was sure that it was all some kind of massive deception. One that she seemed intent on maintaining, even when no-one else was around to observe it. 'Could you help me with some homework Archer? I've got a modular exam coming up and I'm hopeless at physics.'

'Can my ears be deceiving me? You wanting to study on a Saturday night?' Penny was astounded.

Mandy's face was the picture of sincerity as she explained that the careers teacher had said she needed to get a good grade in science if she wanted to try nursing.

'That's a worthwhile career, but it's a lot of hard work.'

'I know, but it's something I have to do. They showed us a film on abused children and it really affected me. I realised how silly I'd been, feeling sorry for myself when there are babies out there suffering terrible things because their parents are junkies or alcoholics. I think I can help because I understand how they feel.'

'It sounds awful, but if it's made you realise there are people out there worse off than you, that's a good thing. I think it's a noble ambition and I'm sure we'll all do everything we can to help you succeed, won't we Archer?'

'Sure. I'd be pleased to help.'

'The exam's not until Friday. My science teacher has given me a revision plan, but I think I'll need to do more than an hour every night to catch up with everything.'

'I'm sure Archer can help, he's good at science.'

'Only if you can spare the time, I know you've got your own work to do.' She seemed to be concerned about someone else apart from herself for the first time since she had been living in the house.

So he came to know a different Mandy, someone with a quick brain and a cynical view of life that made her witty observations on the people around her cruelly accurate. It seemed that she genuinely wanted to study and because many of the topics involved areas of his expertise, they formed a good working relationship. It wasn't just the change in her appearance or motivation to study, she really did seem to become much nicer in her treatment of Archer, no longer trying to impose herself on him physically. She kept a discrete distance away from him as he helped her to study and the only contact was occasional light, friendly gestures like a brief high five or a punch on the shoulder if he teased her. He found himself teasing her more and more lately as he had in his dealings with Rory.

Rory came on Monday, and if she saw any change in her former tormentor's behaviour she made no comment about it. Mandy went out of her way to talk to her. 'Look, I'm sorry if I was rotten to you, there was no excuse really, but I've seen the error of my ways and I'm trying to be a better person. I hope you'll find it within you to forgive me.' She held out her hand but Rory just raised her eyebrows slightly and walked straight past.

Mandy shrugged. 'Oh dear, it looks like I hurt her too deeply.'

Archer tried not to show his concern at Rory's uncharacteristic behaviour. 'I'm sure she'll come round. Maybe she just had a bad day.'

Mandy squeezed his hand demurely. 'That's one of the things I love about you. You refuse to see the bad in anyone, even me.'

They heard the door slam as Rory walked into the kitchen and Mandy jumped.

Twenty Three

'Rory, you made me jump, slamming the door like that.'

'Sorry Aunt Penny, the wind must have caught it.'

Penny frowned, none of the doors or windows were open and there was no wind to speak of. She tried with her normal remedy for the ills of all children. 'Help yourself to a flapjack, they've got a special little surprise.'

'Thank you, but I'd like a cup of chocolate please.'

Raising her eyebrows at the unusual request, Penny switched the kettle on. 'Want to talk about it?'

'No. Yes. I don't know. What does she think she's playing at?'

'Who dear? Has someone been annoying you at school?'

'That ... Mandy. Who does she think she's fooling, dressing all Sandra Dee and acting meek and mild?'

'Dressing all Sandra Dee? You mean because she's not wearing all that war paint and showing off her tattoos?'

'And why a blonde Cinderella wig? I'd have thought Cruella de Ville was more her style.'

'Well all that hair won't grow back straightaway. Maybe she's experimenting with different styles until she finds one that suits her.' Penny poured the boiling water and stirred.

'In that case she'd be head-to-toe in black with blood dripping from her teeth and nails.'

'Eugh, sounds like someone's been watching too many horror movies.' Penny was concerned, she had never seen her little charge so negative about anything or anyone. 'Try not to judge her too harshly my dear, she's been through a hard time of it lately.'

'Hard time is what she gives everyone else.' Rory muttered under her breath and although Penny didn't hear the words, the sentiment was obvious from her expression.

'Well she seems to have turned over a new leaf and is trying really hard. It wouldn't hurt you to show a little mercy and try to forgive whatever she has done to you.'

Rory took a deep breath to calm herself down and blew on the hot drink before taking a sip. So the witch had Aunt Penny fooled, but hopefully Archer would be able to see through her.

Except that he seemed to be under some kind of spell too. In fact, everyone at the table was completely taken in by her. Mandy was utterly convincing in this new role, going from evil brat monster to caring, considerate geek in a heartbeat. There was none of the attention-seeking attitude she displayed on their previous meal together.

She seemed to blend into the background modestly and appeared genuinely interested when Uncle Todd started talking about an incident at the laboratory where he worked. She listened to his tale without interruption or ridicule and asked intelligent questions about what had happened. He seemed to appreciate her attention, saying more than Rory had ever heard him say at one meal time; usually he seemed miles away, probably still at work inside his head.

Rory could tell that Archer's attitude toward Mandy had changed, he was actually starting to like her. Despite his efforts to appear friendly and not to flinch when she touched him, Rory could tell that Archer was not entirely comfortable with her constant stroking and patting when they last ate together. But this time, on the few occasions she accidentally brushed his fingers or knocked his elbow, his body did not cringe away. It was this, finally that gave Rory her first doubts. *Could she be wrong about her? Was it possible that someone with such a black heart could actually turn into a nice person?*

It certainly seemed so, if you believed the evidence of your eyes and ears. Gone was the vicious, self-centred flirt who dressed like a tarty punk. In her place was a humble, generous sweetheart whose outfits would not have looked out of place in church. After three days of nothing but sweetness and light, there was no evidence of any cracks in her façade, she seemed able to maintain this gentle persona with no effort. Rory was a little curious where her new wardrobe had come from, but on the fourth day she started to mix and match the new stuff with items from her old wardrobe, using scarves and a prim little cardigan to cover areas of flesh she would previously have flaunted.

The scary thing was the way she was being nice to Rory, more than just polite, actively taking an interest in her wellbeing. She asked about her day at school, offered her help with her homework and stayed to help when Rory insisted on taking on her share of the chores.

'It's alright, you don't need to help, you did it yesterday.'

'I know, but it doesn't seem right somehow, you're so much younger than everyone else and you're really still a guest who just happens to be staying a few extra days.'

'Well it would be a help, I can't reach the high cupboard without standing on a stool.'

'No problem, I'll get those then. You do the plates and the cutlery.'

Tom finished washing up and disappeared quickly without rinsing off the pots and pans properly, so she did that while Rory did the cutlery.

'How are you holding up without your Mum? Penny was saying she's never been away this long before.'

'I'm fine thank you.'

'You must be missing her though.'

'She rings up every night just before I go to bed and tells me about her day and sends me a goodnight kiss.'

'Ahhh, that's so sweet. It must be nice to have that kind of relationship with your Mum. My Mum couldn't care less about me or Kellie, she never has.'

'She must have done once, when you were little.'

'Nope. She was too busy tarting around. She worked as a barmaid and we never saw her in the evenings.'

'Somebody must have cared about you or you wouldn't have been educated as well as you are.'

Mandy put the last pan away then stood still as the memories took over. 'My gran brought us up then, she was well strict. We hated it at the time, but I guess we've probably got a lot to thank her for.'

Rory finished by wiping down the draining board and kitchen table. 'Thanks for your help.'

'Don't mention it. Any time. Do you really think I'm well educated?'

'Yes. I can tell when you're talking to Archer that you're a lot smarter than you make out. I think you could make it into nursing if that's what you want to do.'

Mandy gave a modest little look. 'It's nice of you to say so, but I don't know if I'm cut out for all that hard work.' She was almost out of the door when she stopped and turned around. 'You never talk about your Dad. Do you ever get to see him?'

A cloud came over Rory's face, spoiling the brief camaraderie they had shared. 'No,' was all she would say. Mandy took the hint and left.

Twenty Four

'Where have you been? I thought we were going to look at those electricity and magnetism questions tonight.'

'Sorry Archer, I was just giving Rory a hand in the kitchen. Don't look at me like that, I didn't think it was fair she should do all the drying up. It was a good job I did, she couldn't reach up to put the glasses away.'

Archer looked back down at the revision guide. He really had heard it all now. Then Rory came out of the kitchen and it was quite obvious that she'd been crying. 'Rory. Are you ok? What's wrong?'

'Nothing.' She ran past them, heading for the stairs.

Dropping the book, he gave Mandy a look that suggested she was responsible and ran after Rory. But when he reached her bedroom, she shut the door. He tapped on the door. 'Rory, it's Archer, let me in.'

'Go away.'

He knocked harder. 'Please Rory. I need to know what happened.'

'Just leave me alone.'

'Only if you open the door and show me you're not hurt.'

There was a minute and then he heard the bed springs creak and soft footsteps padded to the door. She opened it a little way. 'I'm not hurt, I'm just missing my Mum.'

'So Mandy didn't do anything to make you cry?'

'No, she was being really helpful. Can I go now?'

'Sure. Sorry, I was a bit worried, that's all.' She shut the door as he slowly turned away.

'Worried that I'd held her arm over the gas flame? That's what happened to one kid on that film they showed us.' Mandy's voice was low and full of sorrow.

He jumped, his concern for Rory meant that he hadn't heard her approach. 'No, I didn't think that, it's just that you have been pretty horrible to her in the past.'

'And a leopard can't change its spots, right.'

'I don't know what you mean.'

'I mean that no matter how much I try to change into the sort of girl you might like, you still think I'm just a nasty bitch who would bully a ten-year-old.' Despite the bitterness in her tone, she still had not raised her voice much above a whisper.

'That's not true. I know you've been trying hard all week to be a nicer person. I can't believe you were just doing that to impress me. Is that the only reason?'

She looked down at the floor and wouldn't meet his eyes. He waited and she shook her head, ever so slightly. He lifted her chin until she was looking into his eyes and the unshed tears glittered in the dim hall light. 'Good, because I really believed that speech when you said about wanting to help abused children. I was really starting to like the new Mandy.'

One of the tears spilled over and rolled down her cheek and he gently smudged it away with his finger, letting it stay on her soft cheek for a little longer than it needed to get the job done.

'Were you really?' The light sparkled in her eyes.

'Yes.' He looked into them for a while and decided that he liked what he saw there. Somehow, he seemed to have moved closer to her and he could feel her breath on his face. It was a moment outside of time, there was nothing else, no sights or sounds or smells, just the two of them, swaying slightly. Their lips seemed to be drawn together with an irresistible force like two poles on a magnet. Then his lips met hers in a kiss so gentle that he wasn't actually sure they had touched at all. He seemed to over-balance slightly and put his hand on her arm. She did the same.

When Rory's door opened, it was a deafening sound, but her tiny gasp was even louder in his ears, then she shut the door again with a very final click.

The moment was everything Mandy had craved. She had made him kiss her like he really meant it, right under Rory's nose. If it had all been an act, she should have been celebrating her complete and absolute victory over Rory and Archer. But there was none of that. She blushed red and actually looked embarrassed. 'Oh dear, we shouldn't be doing that here. We'd better go.'

'Where to, your room?'

'No.'

'Of course not, Kellie will be there. My room then?'

'No. I – actually, I'm not really that sort of girl at all. It was just a rebellion.'

'Yeah right. So when you put your hand on my thigh you were just looking for …?

'Your hand. I wanted to hold your hand.'

'Right. I believe you. Millions wouldn't.'

She giggled. 'You really must stop watching those old re-runs on TV. Your jokes are sooo old.'

Rory didn't stop long the next day, Lynette had beaten the weekend traffic and picked her up early. Mandy returned from school saying that she had done well on her physics paper and asked Archer to go into town on Saturday. 'I'll buy you a coffee to celebrate.'

'What would be the point? You could make me a coffee here and it wouldn't cost you anything.'

'Because it's a treat. You sit in a café where people serve you cakes and you chat and watch the world go by.'

'I still don't get it, but if it's a treat then yes, we should go because you deserve a treat after all that hard work.'

Although it was much as she had described it, Archer could not for the life of him understand why it was a treat. Sitting on a hard chair at a stained table in an overcrowded room with people pushing past every few minutes was not his idea of fun. It was raining outside, the windows were steamed up so you could not see out and the noise level meant it was difficult to talk. The coffee was lukewarm and foamy and the cake looked like it had been left out since the previous day. It tasted as though it was full of E numbers.

Mandy, however, seemed to be thoroughly enjoying the experience. Looking round, he could see a number of couples holding hands and leaning almost close enough to kiss. But the vast majority of people were women, in twos or threes, with stacks of shopping bags or with a number of children in tow. Cafés were obviously a "girl" thing.

Rory did not come round for the next couple of weeks and things at Penny's settled into a routine. Archer continued to spend much of his time with Mandy; it became a mutual support exercise as she applied brain power to her studies and started listening in lessons. Even Kellie joined in, she would be taking her SATs tests in May in English, maths and science. She was not as bright as Mandy, but she listened while they were talking about the science and joined in with some of the maths.

He was pleasantly surprised when Peter rang up one evening, suggesting that they could meet up on Saturday. 'They've been doing a series of Bond doubles, so you get two movies for the price of one.'

'Bond doubles?'

'I forgot you've been living in the dark ages. James Bond. Double-oh-seven? He's an action hero. Just say "yes Peter I'd love to come".'

'Yes Peter I'd love to come.'

'I'll meet you by the bus station at nine thirty then.'

So began Archer's education in Saturday morning adventure films. To begin with he was embarrassed by the naked girls in the title sequence and the bedroom scenes. He was sceptical of some of the daring feats and he really couldn't get his head round some of the plotting devices. In the interval between Diamonds are Forever and Live and Let Die, he questioned Peter as they stood in the queue to get ice cream. 'So this villain Blofeld did not really die at the beginning in the hot mud, but it was someone pretending to be him.'

'Yeah they altered the faces of some of his henchmen using plastic surgery to make them look like him. It was real science fiction stuff when they made the film in the seventies, but it's quite common now.'

'People wanting to look like other people?'

'No, just wanting to look prettier. They have their nose made smaller or their boobs made bigger.'

'But they wouldn't actually do this surgery, it was just the same actor playing all the parts.'

'Yeah. It's pretty good the way they film it so you can have the same actor twice in the same scene.'

'But there seemed to be a lot of times where the actors are pretending to be different characters, or get mistaken for other characters. It's almost like Shakespeare.'

'I'll take your word for that mate. Come on, we need to get back in for the next one.'

Archer thought that this was a story concerning the same character, but it was played by a completely different actor. Just when he thought he'd understood it, the rules seemed to change again. He wanted to ask Peter about it, but there was a woman in front of them with two young lads. She turned and glared when he asked a question during the first film, so he dare not ask again. It spoilt his concentration, he could not help but compare this man's portrayal of the role to the previous actor who had been much more credible as a tough man of action.

The action did not hold his attention so well, he had little understanding of the ideas of drug-running and Voodoo, which were so fundamental to the plot. He found the idea of using crocodiles, snakes and sharks to kill people upsetting and had to stop himself from laughing out loud at the end when the villain blew up like a balloon and exploded.

As the credits played there was a reprise of the song that opened the movie, it started slow and melodic, but got very noisy. Everyone was leaving, but Peter sat in his seat nodding his head vigorously in time to the music and playing his pretend drums and what he called an air guitar.

'I love this. Guns N' Roses did a cover of it, but I think the original's brilliant.'

'A good name for a rock band.' Archer knew Peter's taste in music.

'Yeah. Will you come again next week?'

'Sure, it was good.'

As he walked home, Archer's thoughts turned to the actors he had seen playing the characters on the screen and how skilfully they had portrayed someone who was totally evil. The actors themselves were probably just like the sort of men you would meet in the street but they were extremely convincing as ruthless cold-blooded killers. It wasn't just men, two of the henchmen in the first movie were played by tall, athletic women who fought like warriors. The thing that stayed in his mind was the way several of the characters had disguised themselves as someone they were not in order to manipulate other people into doing what they wanted them to do.

Twenty Five

The next Saturday saw two more movies with the same actor, Archer was getting used to him and warmed to the way he didn't really take himself seriously; there was always a twinkle in his eye as he delivered the corniest of lines, usually to scantily-clad women. On the following week, Peter was ready to leave at the first credit.

'Don't suppose you wanna go and get a burger or something, I'm starving.'

'Sure, I don't have to get straight back.'

Ten minutes later they were sitting at one of the café tables at the top level of the small shopping mall, looking out over the rest of the town having their weekly retail therapy session. Peter was so hungry that he had virtually finished his burger before they sat down. 'Come on then, tell me all about your new place. What's it like?'

Archer had just taken a huge bite of his burger and he pointed to his full mouth and chewed fast until it was gone. 'Sorry about that, I can't talk with my mouth full. It's horrible.'

'Really? Are they dead strict and nasty to you?'

'No, I'm talking about this food. How can you eat it? It just tastes of cardboard and E numbers.' He tried a chip.

'Waste not want not.' Peter picked it up, opening the batch to take out the slice of gherkin, then ramming half of it into his mouth at once.

'Steady on mate. Has Julie stopped feeding you?'

Peter pointed at his mouth.

'Now you can't talk. It's not too bad. Penny and Todd are stricter than your Mum and Dad, but she's an amazing cook. Not that Julie's bad, but Penny bakes fresh cakes and pies and her muffins are a work of art.'

Peter gulped down the last of his mouthful. 'Sounds good. What about the other kids? I bet you haven't got anyone strapping you to trees and threatening to shoot arrows at you.'

'Funny you should say that...' Archer took another chip then slid the box over, they were equally inedible.

'No, really? Do you want us to sort them out?'

'Nah, I was only joking. There's only one other lad Tom, he's only thirteen but he's pretty cool.'

'Is that it? Just the two of you?'

'No. Rory comes once a week, Mandy and Kellie...'

'I thought you said there was only one boy.'

'Rory's short for Aurora. She's only twelve, but she's pretty smart. Taught me how to do algebra.'

'So that's it. You're stuck with a bunch of little kids. That must be tame after us lot.'

'It certainly isn't tame. Kellie's fourteen and Mandy's sixteen and they both know how to cause trouble.'

'Are they fit?'

'I don't know, I've never seen them run or do anything sporting. I suppose they must be reasonably fit, neither of them is carrying any extra weight.'

'No I mean fit as in hot. Pretty face, good body, nicely presented.'

'I don't know. When I first got there, they both wore far too much make-up. Kellie is a goth, all pale face and head-to-toe black, but you would probably think she's quite cute. Mandy is – was a punk. Lots of tight leather and tattoos and a bright pink Mohican.'

'Sounds like a girl Jack was hanging out with. I haven't seen her lately though.'

'Really. When was the last time he saw her?'

Peter shrugged, looking down at the ground. 'Dunno.'

'Think Peter, this could be important. If it is the same girl … could you ask him for me?'

'I dunno. I don't see much of him these days.'

Archer narrowed his eyes, sensing there was more to come and watched Peter playing with the last few chips.

'I wish you'd come back, you made such a difference to everyone. I was starting to like the atmosphere in the house, but now it's back to normal and people are just fighting and bitching at each other all the time.'

'You mean Jack and Kyle?'

'Yes, but it's not just them. Dad always seems to be having a go at Mum for something and she's not letting him get away with it anymore.'

'What do you mean?' Archer cleared the rubbish.

'She stands up to him when he treats her like a slave and tells him to get his own beer if she's busy.'

'That's a good thing isn't it?'

'I guess so. We're all supposed to give a hand with the clearing up after meals, but Dad walks away and the others copy him. So mostly it's just me and her. Now you pointed it out, I don't think it's fair she should do it all, but I don't think it's fair the others get away with it either.'

'There's a standard answer for that where I come from. "Life's not fair." Someone usually answers, "And then you die." I'm sure she appreciates that you're doing your bit to help.'

'Yeah. She says sometimes it's only me that's keeping her sane, making her life worth living.'

'Oh dear, that doesn't sound good.'

'I know. She's gone all tree-hugger like Aunty Dawn, saying we've got to recycle all the bottles and paper. She goes mad if we throw away a carrier bag.'

'Don't hate me, but that could be my fault. I was telling her what it was like where I lived and how much energy it takes to make paper and glass. We re-use everything.'

'I've been reading some scary stories about what the world will be like only fifty years from now. That's like when my kids would be grown up.'

'Always assuming some girl will marry you.'

'Cheeky buggar. The internet says it'll be dire if we don't do something to reduce our waste and stop wrecking the ozone layer.'

'We need to stop wasting the earth's resources every day, every person. But I can't see it happening anytime soon. No-one wants to give up central heating, their car or individually wrapped chocolate bars.'

'You really think it needs to go that far?'

'That's not nearly far enough. Anyway, this punk girl Jack knows. Is he going out with her?'

'I don't know. We had a big bust up a few weeks ago and I haven't seen much of him since.'

'What happened?'

'It's quite a long story. You haven't got to get back anytime soon have you?'

'Just give me the highlights.'

'You know we were supposed to be being really good at school in case Barston sent the social workers poking around at Mum and Dad's?'

'Did anything happen about that?'

'All in good time. They were good as gold at the start, especially Jack, he was getting lots of blue slips. I got some and a couple of praise postcards sent home.'

'Sounds promising.'

'Dad gave us all some money to celebrate in town so we went to see the first Bond double. They didn't like Dr No, said it was too old fashioned, so they went to the mall instead of watching the next one.' He took a sip of his coke. 'They met Brett and I assumed they were just mooching round the shops. Jack mentioned a girl with a pink Mohican. I don't know what they were doing, but the next week I went on my own.'

'You should have called me back then.'

'I wish I had. When I got home Jack asked to see my ticket. I showed him and he said "Thanks mate" and walked off with it. I asked him to give it back because I'm making a scrap book of all the Bond stuff. He said he needed it, but he'd give it back eventually.'

Archer looked at his ticket. 'Why would he only want it for a little while? That doesn't make sense.'

'That's what I thought. Anyway he seemed all twitchy and Kyle said something like "what about me?" Jack told him to shut up and listen. Then he asked me about the films, who was in them and what happened. I told them the outline, but he was asking lots of questions and I didn't know the answers. He got annoyed and asked if I actually watched the film. It seemed important that he knew all the details so I suggested he looked it up on the internet.'

'Weird. Why didn't he just come and watch them if he wanted to know what they were about?'

'He didn't.'

'But you just said …'

'I know. Then he asked me where I was sitting in the theatre and how many other people were in there.'

'How would he expect you to know that? You would have been watching the film not counting how many people were sitting in there with you.'

'That's exactly what I said. He said he didn't mean exactly, just was it full or empty.'

'Why would he want to know that? And what's that got to do with the film?'

'Then he asked me what time it started and finished and how long the interval was and I finally started putting two and two together. Look at your ticket again.'

Archer looked at the ticket closely, then turned it over and looked at the other side. There was just an advert for the website so he turned it back and it finally clicked. 'Of course. So what did you do?'

'What could I do? I let him have the ticket and said nothing, but I kept my ear to the ground just in case.'

'In case of what?'

'In case I might end up in big trouble.'

Twenty Six

Archer was in familiar territory. Much of his recent life was a series of dilemmas, all of which had two equally tough alternatives both with horrendous consequences. Except in this case there was a third alternative – *a trilemma?* – which possibly had the least honour, but could be safest in the long run.

The one that would be the hardest and cause the most personal pain would be to confront the individuals involved. He discussed with Peter what the crime might be, but they hadn't come up with anything concrete. The lack of solid evidence meant that any confrontation would be fraught with problems. It would be too easy for the perpetrators to wriggle out of it or they might react violently, because violence was definitely one of their preferred modes of operation. There was the tiniest possibility that they were completely innocent, but given the nature of the characters involved, that was unlikely.

It was this faint chance that stopped Archer from choosing the second alternative, to hand the problem over to an adult, someone in authority who could deal with it properly. This option had less immediate personal risk, and the advantage that trained professionals would be able to get to the truth quickly and impersonally.

So in the short term, he took the third option which was to say absolutely nothing to anyone, but to watch out for the slightest clue. This meant he had to act as though he was ignorant of what had gone on and was still totally taken in by their performances. The warrior training helped, his ability to assume the cold face was useful. But it wasn't enough to suppress his natural revulsion to the evil that lurked just below the surface. He had to continue to behave as though he was infatuated with the reformed Mandy. Which meant he had to ignore Rory as much as possible or act as though she was an annoying little brat.

When he met Peter on Saturday, he was no further on in solving the mystery as they tried a different café.

'Apart from the fact that she's wearing more new clothes, I don't have much of a clue.'

'Well I have. You know we said that Jack must have needed the ticket for some kind of alibi.'

'So he could pretend he was watching Bond movies all afternoon.' Archer tried the Cornish pasty Peter had recommended; it was much more like real food.

'When did Mandy change her appearance?'

Archer told him the date and he worked out the number of weeks since then. 'Yep. That fits exactly. That's the week Jack asked for the ticket. Has she suddenly got any other new gear?'

'I already told you about the new clothes.'

Peter was about to explain, then caught Archer's grin. 'I mean a Game Boy or new videos like Indiana Jones.'

'Yeah, she said her Discman was broken and now she's using it again. And I saw her with a stack of new CDs.'

'Well you know those plastic anti-theft devices they put round the CDs and videos to stop people nicking them? I found a load of them at the back of the garage.'

'No. You didn't touch them did you?' Archer had taken a liking to the many different detective shows on TV.

'And get my fingerprints all over them? I'm not completely stupid. They were tucked away in a box under the workbench hidden by some old pictures. I don't know how long they had been there. Not very long, there was no dust. I put it back exactly as I found it.'

'Good thinking.'

'I reckon they grabbed a load and set the alarm off. They were probably recognised or something.'

'That's why she's stopped wearing the pink Mohican.'

'Otherwise the next time she went into town people would recognise her.'

'Maybe they planned it like that. One group of kids looks pretty much the same as any other group.'

'A goth or two, a couple of punks and lots of denim and shell suits.' Peter was looking at the kids on a table across the room. 'So a pink Mohican would catch people's attention and they wouldn't notice much else.'

'Exactly. I bet the others all wore something unusual on that day and they just went for broke.'

'Of course. Jack was in this foul green and black shell suit. I'd never seen it before, it was brand new but it was like he'd been rolling round in the mud in it. Next day I saw it in the dustbin. He said it got wrecked and he hated it anyway.'

'So that's no use as evidence. But very memorable.'

'I think so. Then suddenly he's got Final Fantasy on the Game Boy and Sonic the Hedgehog for the Mega Drive.'

'It all fits. But what are we going to do about it?'

Twenty Seven

Rory found the evidence that confirmed the scam when Penny asked her to collect the dirty mugs and glasses from the girls' bedroom.

'But they don't like me going up there. I don't want her shouting at me again.'

'They won't know it was you, they're at their gran's tonight. If she asks, I'll say I collected them. You will be doing me a big favour, it will take two or three trips, there must be twenty up there.'

'Alright. I'll take a tray to help me to carry more.'

'I don't like the idea of you carrying a full tray down the stairs. Archer, will you give her a hand?'

'Sure.' He'd never been up in their domain before, and might find something incriminating. As they reached the landing, he realised this was the first time he'd been alone with Rory since Mandy's image change. He felt he should say something, but didn't know what. The sentences he was constructing in his head were forgotten as he was assaulted by the chaos of their room. 'How can they live like this?' Every surface was covered in an untidy mess of clothes, magazines, make-up, dirty mugs and plates.

'I don't know. I'm surprised they don't catch something. The place is probably teeming with mice.'

'What a mess. How can they find anything?' He picked up a couple of mugs that looked like they were growing something Todd could have used in his lab.

'Watch out. I've just found a mug half-filled with cold tea. And lots of the glasses have still got water in them.'

'We could empty them, before we take them down.'

'No, I'll wash them up. Aunt Penny's busy enough.'

'Good idea. I'll wipe then. If there's such a thing as a clean tea towel.'

'It's about the only thing in here that is clean. Probably never been used.'

Archer laughed. He had forgotten how witty her dry observations could be. As he lifted a mug, a pile of precariously balanced books toppled to the floor. Picking them up, a cover caught his eye, showing a very suspicious looking young woman in a clothes shop on the front. The caption read, "She just couldn't stop herself." He read the words on the back and his eyes widened. It was a book about a girl who stole things from shops. A shoplifter. He opened it and started to read.

'Good book is it?' Rory's comment made him jump. Why don't you sit down and make yourself comfortable while I finish up here?'

'Sorry, I was curious. I've never heard of a shoplifter.'

'I wondered where that had got to. Mum gave it to me, but it's a teen romance, far too slushy and I didn't like the girl, she was weak and spoilt.'

'So why did she steal things?'

'To get attention. Her parents were splitting up and they were too wrapped up in their own problems to notice her.'

'Sounds familiar.'

'Well there's no excuse for her taking it out of my room without asking. I would have lent it to her if she'd asked, but she's no business being in my room.'

'So she stole this book. Pretty ironic really.'

'Because she stole a book about stealing.'

'Exactly.'

'She was probably going to give it back eventually.'

'How can you be so nice about her when she's been so horrible to you?'

'Not lately she hasn't. She's been quite nice to me. Ever since you've been going out with her.'

'I'm not going out with her. We went out once and had a cup of foam and a plate full of E numbers.'

Rory laughed. 'But Tom says you've been out every Saturday for hours and so has she.'

'I've been going to the cinema with my mate Pete. I've no idea where she's been.' He held up the book. 'No that's a lie. I have a pretty good idea where she's been going and what she's been doing.'

'What, you mean she's been stealing things?'

'Take a look around. Did they have this much stuff when they came?'

Rory shrugged. 'I don't know. I wasn't here. I have noticed them wearing a lot of new clothes lately. You don't think ...?' She pointed to the book. 'There's a bit in the book where it describes how the girl did it with her friend. But of course. Kellie.'

'I don't think it's just clothes or that it was only the two of them. A couple of foster lads at Pete's house have been coming home with all sorts of new videos and computer games, even a new Game Boy.'

'Her Discman was broken I bet it's here somewhere.' Rory started looking in cupboards and drawers.

'Careful. Don't move anything except mugs and stuff.'

'Look at this.' At the back of the wardrobe there was a plastic bag with a couple of cheap and nasty looking shell suits in pastel colours and a short black wig.

'So that's how she's doing it. She leaves here with a blonde wig and changes into this gear before they start stealing. I wonder where they go to change?'

'Most of the shops have changing rooms or she could use the ladies toilets.'

'Possibly. It would have to be somewhere they could leave all the gear though.

'Maybe a friend's house. Does Pete live near town?'

'Not really, but from what he's saying there's more than four of them.'

'You could follow them one week and find out.'

It all worked out perfectly, the next week was half term, and the cinema was taken over with wall-to-wall Disney films. That meant that Peter and Archer could give the impression they were going to the movies as normal and have a reasonable excuse for being at the shopping mall when the others got there. Peter walked into town with the other boys, then left them to meet Archer by the bus station. Crossing the busy road, he saw the direction they took and followed at a safe distance on the other side of the street. They walked for five minutes, taking a left turn and he crossed over and watched as they knocked on the door of a terraced house. The girl that opened the door was wearing a lilac shell suit and, from that distance, looked as though her head was completely shaved. As she turned he saw a stripe of hair down the back of her head, all that remained of the pink Mohican.

There was a large building opposite the house with a notice giving a list of the doctors and the opening times. At the bottom in big black letters it said "**SURGERY CLOSED SATURDAY AND SUNDAY**." He slipped into the garden, crouched behind a hedge and waited. Five minutes later Jack came out with the girl in the lilac shell suit, now wearing a short black wig. His denim jacket and jeans were replaced by a pale green shell suit. A goth girl was next, her long black skirt reaching almost to the floor. Kyle came out then with two others that Peter didn't know, all of them dressed in jeans and bland jackets that would blend easily into any crowd. He watched until they were out of sight, then waited a few minutes more. Crossing the street, he made a note of the house number, then ran to meet Archer. 'Sorry I'm late. I followed them to a house in Tower Street and that Mandy girl was there, she's had the Mohican trimmed and she's wearing a black wig. They went towards the mall.'

'Was Kellie there?'

'Is that the goth girl?'

'Yeah.' They started walking to the mall.

'Is she a lot fatter than Mandy?'

'No, they're about the same size. Why?'

'There was a goth girl but she looked twice the size of Mandy. It could just have been the layers of black scarves and things.'

'Or it could be part of their scheme.' Archer explained the trick used in Rory's book. As they got to the mall they agreed to split up and check one floor each, meeting back in ten minutes in the bookshop near the entrance, hoping that this was not the sort of shop the others would go to.

Archer got back first and pretended to look at the books in the big display of new titles. He picked one up and was reading the back cover when Peter arrived, out of breath as though he had been running.

'You'd better come quick, they've split up but Mandy and Jack are in the music shop. I think it's about to kick off.'

Twenty Eight

By the time they got there, Jack and Mandy were going down the escalators, she had a large bag from the music store. After a hurried conversation, Peter followed Jack as he headed towards the men's toilets. Archer watched as Mandy went into one of the largest clothing stores, picked up four items and headed for the changing rooms. There was a boy sitting on a seat outside the changing room who looked vaguely familiar. After staring at him for a second, he realised it was Kyle, but he looked a lot fatter. It was a good disguise with spectacles, his hair gelled flat and the bulk from several extra jumpers under his jacket. He must have felt someone was staring at him as he turned round. The guilty look on his face told Archer that he was definitely involved in this thing.

'Hi Kyle, nearly didn't recognise you. How are you?'

'Fine thanks. How are you?'

'I'm good. Are you still getting those blue slips?'

Kyle snorted in derision. 'As if. It was great for the first week or so, we were being really good and trying hard like you said. Lots of teachers were pleased and saying good things. Jack even got a praise postcard sent home and Peter got a couple.'

'That's great.'

'It didn't last. Barston decided we were forging them and he made the teachers sign a sheet in his office every time they gave us a blue slip. The teachers don't have time to do that, so they stopped bothering.'

'That's terrible. Don't tell me you stopped working.'

'Not straight away. The deputy head started showing up on our patch at break and lunch, looking for any excuse to give us a yellow slip. Jack got one for not wearing his tie because we were late back from PE and he went to get his lunch first.'

'Doesn't sound very fair.'

'Too right it wasn't very fair. It was like he wanted to prove that we were a pair of thugs.'

'Not Pete then.'

'No, he never seemed to get picked on and the teachers were still giving him blue slips. Oops, gotta go. See you around.'

Archer turned to see Kellie coming out of the changing room and watched the woman count her four items, then Mandy's four. He only recognised Mandy because of the shell suit and the black wig. She was wearing a lot of make-up and looked as though she was a bit fatter, but nothing like as much as Kellie.

'Mandy? Why are you dressed like that?'

She turned round and looked at him with faint curiosity as though she was wondering why he was talking to her, then grabbed Kellie's arm and the pair of them walked down toward the exit. When they were out of sight of the dressing room attendant, they put all four hangers back on the nearest rail. As they approached the door there was a boy wearing an expensive leather jacket and the three of them went out together setting off all the alarms. It was cleverly done, the security guard came up and the girls lifted their hands to show they weren't carrying anything and the boy said sorry, he had just wanted to have a look at the colour of the jacket in daylight. As the man dealt with him, the other two walked off towards the ladies toilets. When they came out five minutes later, Mandy looked her normal size and both girls had several carrier bags. Archer watched as Kyle came up and had a quick word with them, they looked around uncertainly then disappeared towards the mall exit.

Archer and Peter had agreed to return to Tower Street and hide in the surgery garden twenty minutes after they split up or if they lost sight of the people they were watching. The girls had obviously decided to go straight back and Archer tailed them on the other side of the street. He reached the surgery and Peter pulled him behind the hedge just as the door opened and Jack's worried face appeared, looking up and down the street as they dived in.

'What do we do now?' Peter sounded concerned. 'We should tell someone.'

Archer went through the options as he saw them, but he was no longer convinced about which one to take. He explained what Kyle had said about the blue slips.

'That's not fair!' Peter was furious. 'No wonder they've been acting all strange. I couldn't think what I'd done to make them avoid me.'

'I think there may be a fourth option.' Archer explained his idea, but they would have to act fast.

Archer knocked on the door and heard voices in the hall. 'Where have you ...? Archer. What are you doing here?'

'Trying to stop you lot from getting into serious trouble. Aren't you going to ask me in Jack?'

'But this is Darren's house.'

'Do his parents know what you get up to?'

'They're at work. Look, this is none of your business.'

'It is my business when friends of mine have turned to crime.'

Just then Kyle came running in. 'Bloody hell, that was close. I'm not doing this again.' He chucked a bag on the floor and a brand new pair of trainers fell out.

'You dork, they're both for the left foot. What a waste of space.'

'Don't blame me, Darren nicked them. But one of the assistants saw him and started a chase. He chucked the bag in the bushes and I picked it up and started running. Isn't he back yet?'

This was even better, they would be much more likely to listen to Archer's suggestion if someone had nearly been caught. Mandy came out of a room off the hallway, complaining that the black wig was too itchy and she didn't want to use it again. She went white when she saw him. 'Archer. What are you doing here?'

'I've come to talk to you about this, you must know it's wrong.' He turned to Jack, the disappointment clear on his face. 'I thought you were trying to change for the better.'

'That's easy for you to say Archer, but you don't know what it's like with Bar-stard and all the teachers getting at you all the time. They call you stupid and tell you you're a waste of space.' Jack was angry at the system that was failing him.

'I spoke to Kyle. I don't think all the teachers are trying to make out you're bad, just the head.'

'Yeah, I suppose you're right.'

'But if you don't stop this now, you will all be caught and sent to some kind of juvenile detention centre.'

'Says who?' A solid, hard-faced boy came out of the room. He was one of the two Archer didn't know.

'Stiff, this is Archer, he's a foster kid too.' Jack seemed to be frightened of this older boy.

'So why is he threatening to rat on his own kind then?'

Archer looked at his watch. 'You have five minutes before the police get here. They will arrest all of you.'

'What? You little bastard, I'm going to smash your face in. Hold him boys.'

Archer knew a moment's doubt as Jack and Kyle both moved to grab his arms. Kellie screamed as Stiff pulled back his arm to deliver the first punch.

Twenty Nine

Archer could not believe that the two boys he thought of as friends were prepared to help this bully to hurt him. Maybe he had completely misjudged them and they were as black-hearted as everyone made them out to be. Help came from an unexpected ally as Mandy grabbed the boy's arm and stepped in between them.

'For God's sake Stiff, think. If he's right about the police you don't have time for this. And the little turd is such a good boy that he probably would have called them. You need to get going.'

'But this was a good little earner and that bastard's ruined it all.'

'No it wasn't. Kyle nearly got caught and Darren probably has, he's not back yet. If you make a mess of his face and the filth get you, it'll be a GBH charge as well. This time they'll just throw away the key. You need to get lost now.'

'You're right as always Mand. I'll catch up with you tomorrow. And you...' he poked his finger in Archer's face, 'I'll be dealing with you later.'

There was a loud banging on the front door and everybody froze except Stiff who ran out of the back door.

'Quick, everyone, give me the bags and I'll get rid of them.' They all jumped to follow Archer's suggestion.

'Right you lot sit down like you're watching telly and I'll stall them as long as I can.' Mandy was in charge and as the thumping began again, she called out, 'Hold on a minute, I'm coming.'

It couldn't have worked out better. Archer ran out the back and down the alleyway between the back gardens, reaching the end just as Pete got there. 'Did they see you?'

'No. After the second time I scarpered, just like you said. My heart is thumping though. Did you get it all?'

'I think so. It's a good job Darren didn't come back or it might not have worked so well. Are you sure you want to do this? There's a big chance you might get caught.'

'As long as we stick to the story we'll be fine. If you're not by the bus stop in half an hour I'll just go home and call you later.'

They split the bags up between them, Peter took the clothes and Archer took the music store bag and the trainers. He had no problem in the music store, he just walked to the counter and left the bag on the end, the assistants were so busy they didn't notice him. When he got to the sports shop a male assistant was watching him closely, so he decided to use their alternative story. He approached the counter.

'I found this bag in the bushes, I think someone might have dropped it.'

The assistant opened the bag and took out the trainers and the man grabbed Archer's arm. 'Would you mind coming with me?' He picked up the bag and led him into the manager's office where a grim looking man was on the telephone. 'Police please. We've caught one of the shoplifting gang. Thank you.'

Thirty

Rory was enjoying herself. Penny spent every fourth Saturday making cartons for the home-made cookies she sold in various shops around the area. Lynette timed her visits for that day and the three of them sat around the big kitchen table bending and folding the cardboard cut-outs to produce a month's supply of empty cartons.

There was always a jolly atmosphere, Penny was a fan of musicals and they would join in with the songs as they worked. There was a constant supply of homemade lemonade and ginger biscuits or fresh fruit muffins. When they finished, Lynette and Penny caught up with the gossip as she baked and Rory usually curled up with a good book or a video. She fell asleep watching Sleeping Beauty, dreaming of Archer fighting a huge dragon with Mandy's face and pink scales all the way down the spine.

The room was dark when she woke up, the TV had switched off when the video ended and it was dark outside. She could hear voices as the girls walked past her, they obviously didn't realise she was there.

'What do you think happened to him?'

'I don't know. First Darren, then Archer. It could have been us.' Mandy sounded worried.

'If the police have got him, do you think he'll tell?'

'Darren? Probably.'

'No Archer.'

'Dunno. It was his own fault for sticking his nose in.'

'D'you think Stiff would have smashed his face ...'

Rory didn't hear the rest of Kellie's question as the door closed behind them, but she was worried. It was her idea that Peter and Archer follow the others and it sounded like was in danger of being beaten up or caught by the police. She needed to find out more. Sliding the door open quietly, she crept up the stairs, following them as they went up to their attic. Holding her breath, she climbed the creaky staircase until she could hear them again.

'… your fault. If Stiff hadn't got such a thing for you it wouldn't have happened. This is the first place we've really had a chance to do well and now it's all ruined. I thought you liked Archer.'

'I did Kellie. I mean I do. Really like him. He's so different to other boys, foster or not. But it was too late, we'd already planned the first run before we met him.'

'I know. You can't say no to Stiff or he'd hurt you.'

'I'm not afraid of that bully, but when I tried to tell him we weren't going to do it anymore, he said he'd hurt you Kell, and I can't 'ave that. You're my baby sis and the only one in this whole world that I trust.'

'Oh Mand, what are we gonna do?' Kellie sounded like she was close to tears.'

'What can we do? If Archer tells then we'll be split up for sure. I'll have to go back to the home and you'll be sent to some really strict place where they hit you if you look the wrong way.'

'I wish we'd never met that prat, he always ruins everything. What do you think Jack will do?'

Rory didn't hear the answer as her Mum called her name and she jumped so much she almost fell.

'Shhhh. Did you hear that? Someone's out there.'

'Maybe he's come back.'

Rory scrambled down the stairs, running into her Mum who laughed in surprise. 'Mum, Archer's in trouble. He tried to catch a gang of shoplifters and he's been caught instead. We need to do something.'

'What? Slow down Rory, I don't understand. Start from the beginning.'

But the telephone rang then and Penny answered it. They stopped and listened to the one-sided conversation. 'Yes, this is she. Police? What...? Yes, full name Don Archer. What now? But my husband … Alright, I'll get there somehow. I'm sure there's been a mistake. Goodbye.'

She turned with an expression of complete shock on her face. 'That was the police. Archer's been caught shoplifting. They want me to go down and answer some questions. Can you give me a lift?'

'Sure. Rory must come, I can't leave her on her own.'

'Oh no, the girls.'

'They'll be fine. When is Todd due back?'

'Any minute now.'

'Don't worry then, they're old enough to look after themselves for a few minutes.'

'What if they run away?'

'Don't be silly Rory, why would they do that?'

'Because …' she wanted to tell everything, but she promised Archer to say nothing. '… they are bad girls.'

'Oh Rory, I know they were a bit troublesome when they first came here, but they've really been trying hard lately. I'm sure they'll be fine.'

The police station was the scariest place Rory had ever been, with a stern-looking man behind a glass screen. She looked around the waiting room while Aunt Penny and her Mum spoke to him. There were several posters shouting their messages at the tops of their voices: **THINK, DON'T DRINK!** and **CLUNK CLICK EVERY TRIP!** She was trying to read about a missing dog when the old man sitting in front of it leaned down and cackled in her face. 'Spare me a pound young miss. I need to buy some medicine.' He breathed all over her and there was a horrible stale smell that made her want to be sick.

'Come here Rory,' called her Mum and she was happy to go and escape his attention. Aunt Penny had to sign a form and then she went round to a side door which opened with a loud buzzing noise.

Lynette sat down on one of the chairs, sighing as she picked up a magazine. 'See if there's something you can read, sweetheart, we're going to be here for a while.'

Rory chose a glossy magazine with a picture of Lady Diana on the front. As she passed by the man, he stretched out his legs and she skipped around them so she didn't trip up, she was sure he had done it deliberately. She gave him a hard stare and sat on the seat on the other side of her Mum, echoing her Mum's sigh as she opened the magazine and looked for the story about Princes William and Harry.

Thirty One

Archer looked around the small dark room with some concern. It was one thing to imagine being caught and carted off to jail, it was quite another to be firmly escorted into a car and left for hours on your own. It gave him plenty of time to think about what he'd done and whether it was right. He worried whether Peter had been caught and if he would be strong enough to say nothing when they asked questions. This concern was interrupted by an image of the shop manager making him wonder why the man had lied to the police, saying that the shop assistant had caught Archer trying to take the trainers out of the shop. This triggered a replay of the last couple of hours.

The burly policemen maintained a firm grip on Archer's arm all the way out to the police car to stop him running away. When they got to the car, he put his hand on Archer's head and pushed him onto the back seat, then got in beside him. The policewoman got into the front and drove to the station where Archer had to fill out a form. They didn't seem very happy about the fact that he was only sixteen, it meant they had to get a parent or legal guardian. When they found out he lived in a foster home, he watched their expressions reflect their opinions of foster kids. At that point, he was brought to the small room and left on his own for an hour, apart from a brief interruption when a lady brought him a white foam cup with something lukewarm and sweet that she called tea.

Finally Penny came in, looking grim face and she hugged him, asking if he was alright.

'No physical contact, please sit down. We have some questions so we can decide if you need to be formally charged.' This man was not dressed in uniform like the other policemen and seemed very serious as he explained the procedure. 'I will write down your answers and this will form part of your statement. Do you understand?'

He nodded. He answered the first few questions truthfully, saying that he usually met Pete on Saturdays to watch movies but they weren't on this week so they went into town instead. The man wrote down Pete's details and said he would be contacted to confirm Archer's story.

Archer told him they'd hung out in town for a while. They spotted the bag in the bushes but Pete had to go home so he took it back to the shop.

'What made you take it back to the shop?'

'I thought if someone had lost it, they might expect it to be handed in at the shop.'

'That's honest. Do you know what was in the bag?'

'Trainers.'

'And you didn't think of taking them for yourself?'

'There wouldn't be much point. They were both for the left foot.'

'Really?' He turned to the man in uniform by the door. 'Can you bring them in here please?' He made a note on the sheet and Penny smiled encouragingly.

'So you say that you were taking them back. Can you tell me about that please?'

Archer described how the man had followed him to the counter and when the woman had taken out the trainers, he had grabbed him and taken him to the manager's office.

'You're saying that a female assistant saw you bring them in. Can you describe her?'

'She was about the same height as Penny, in her thirties, slim, short curly brown hair, brown eyes and her name tag said Brenda.'

'Whoa, hold on. Brown hair, brown eyes, Brenda. Well that's a comprehensive description young man, we should be able to find her from that. If her statement agrees with yours, it puts a different slant on the matter. Now is there anything else you can tell me about this incident?'

'Nothing. I don't know why the man lied about me trying to take the trainers. I would never steal anything.'

The man stared hard and Archer held his gaze steady, knowing that apart from a few details, most of his tale was the truth and that his intention was pure.

'Well I must say you look like the sort of boy that has been brought up to be decent and honest. I hope when we get statements from the staff at the shop, this friend of yours,' he looked at his notes, 'Peter and your head teacher, you will be cleared and the matter closed.'

'I'm sure he did not commit any crime. Archer is a good boy and he works hard. He's an excellent influence on the other foster children.'

'I'm sure he is Mrs Gardner. The constable will show you out and we'll be in touch when we find out more.'

Rory hugged him when they walked into the waiting room and he whirled her round and put her down, breathless and laughing. 'I knew they'd let you out. You couldn't steal anything, you're much too honest.'

They had to get back to the girls so they hurried out to the car, everyone talking loudly with Rory and Lynette both asking questions at the same time. Penny finally had enough. 'Let him get his breath back, I'm sure he'll tell you the whole story when we get home.'

When they walked in, Todd was sitting in the kitchen reading the paper, totally unaware of any problems.

Penny's concern took over. 'Are the girls alright?'

'I don't know. I thought they were with you.'

'Rory, would you be a dear and check they're ok? Tell them the dinner's going to be a little late and ask if they would like a cup of tea while they're waiting.'

They were on their way down and Mandy seemed to be innocence itself as Rory relayed her Aunt's question. 'We were wondering if Penny needed a hand with the dinner, it's usually ready by now.'

Rory didn't believe a word, she was sure they just wanted to hear whether he'd given the police their names or not. Aunt Penny seemed pleased with their offer.

'I'm sorry girls. I know we don't usually do this, but it's been an unusual day. I'm going to order a take-out, is everyone happy with Chinese? I'll get a mix of dishes and we can all share.'

She disappeared out to the other room with the leaflet as Lynette poured the tea. Everyone sat round the kitchen table as Archer retold his tale. Except that Rory knew it was an edited version, he didn't mention anything about the girls apart from the fact that he'd seen them in the shop. When he said about the police writing down Peter's details, Kellie went even paler than normal, but Mandy was quite calm. 'Did you give the police our details as well?'

'Why would I do that? They already have this address.'

'Didn't you tell them you saw us in town?' She saw the curious looks Todd and Lynette were giving her and added, 'I was just wondering whether the police might need to ask us to back up Archer's story. Which we would do, of course.'

'No, I don't think I mentioned that I saw you in town.'

'Nor Jack and Kyle?'

Archer knew exactly what she was worried about and looked at her for a couple of seconds before replying. 'Now I come to think about it, I don't think I said anything at all, just that I was hanging out with Pete. But you could be right, it might be worth telling them I saw you guys, maybe I should ring them now.'

The horror on her face was brief and she started to protest before she realised he was winding her up, but by then it was too late, Todd had picked up on it. 'Actually, that might not be a bad idea, what do you think dear?'

Penny had just returned from phoning through the order. 'I think I've had enough of police stations for one day, they'll only make him go down again to write it all out and sign it. I'm sure he'll be fine. When they get the statements from the shop assistants and the head teacher, they'll realise he is innocent and it will all be over.'

But she couldn't have been more wrong. It was as though the fates were conspiring against Archer in every possible way. Brenda, the one witness who could have made a difference, had finished her shift half an hour after the incident. She left with her boyfriend for a week's holiday in France and her family had no idea where she was staying. Peter's statement backed Archer's up in every detail, but he was only sixteen and they were friends, so it didn't carry much weight in the scheme of things.

Although the head at his current school had given him a good report, a particularly zealous young detective spotted that he had previously been at another school. Mr Barston viewed this as a chance for revenge on the boy that had been so cheeky and then disappeared out of reach of his circle of power.

The manager of the shoe shop was extremely annoyed by the number of thefts from his store in recent months. Calling in the male assistant that had brought Archer to him, he gave him two choices. He made it quite clear that a message needed to be sent out to "the thieving scum" that there was a penalty for stealing from his store. And that if the right message was not sent out, his job would be in jeopardy. If the message was clear, there may be a bonus involved.

So when the detective inspector in charge of the case put all of this evidence together, he decided that there was sufficient cause for a more detailed investigation and a letter was sent informing Penny that Don Archer would need to present himself at the juvenile court on the following Thursday for an initial hearing.

Thirty Two

'You can not be serious. That's not fair.'

'How can they possibly get away with that?'

'I'm sorry boys. I think it's completely unjustified.' Julie tried to calm Jack and Kyle down as they reacted to the news. 'You've both been doing so well at school and been so helpful round the house. I think it's terrible that this should come through now.'

'But it's not fair that they blame you guys and try to take your licence away because we were bad six months ago.' Jack looked ready to punch something.

'That's the trouble with bureaucracy, it always takes so long.' Julie was startled by the sound from the hallway of the 'phone slamming down. Peter stormed in.

'It didn't take them long to decide Archer was guilty, they're sending him to court next week.'

'What? You are joking. Peter, tell me you are joking.'

'No Jack, it's such a pile of …'

'Peter. There must be a mistake, Archer wouldn't do anything illegal, he's not like that.'

'He didn't. He found some trainers that some toe-rags,' Peter looked hard at the other two who were staring open-mouthed, 'had stolen. He tried to return them to the shop.'

'But surely the assistant …'

'Gone on holiday.'

'Well there must be something I can do. A character reference or something.'

'From someone whose foster licence is under question? That's not going to help much.' Jack was brutally honest.

'But they can't send him down. Someone else must have seen him try to return them.' Kyle was desperate.

'The other assistant and manager are lying. And guess which headmaster got do some character assassination.'

'Not Bar-stard? This can't be happening. Poor Archer. This is all our fault. We've got to do something.' Kyle was pacing round angrily, directing his anger at Jack.

Julie was surprised and touched by their loyalty. 'Look Kyle, it's not your fault if the head's got it in for him – for all of us. Try to calm down. I'll ring Penny and find out what's going on and if there's anything we can do.'

When she left the room, Peter turned on them. 'I hope you two are pleased with yourselves. After everything he tried to do for you, Archer is prepared to carry the can.'

'I know, you don't need to tell me. Mandy's been giving me earache, saying we should own up, or at least drop Stiff in it. It was all his idea in the first place.'

'I dunno why you're so afraid of him. He's just a boy.'

'That's because you've never been in a children's home Peter. It's a real jungle and only the strongest survive.'

'I suppose this Stiff character was lord of that jungle.'

'He was so much more than that. Nobody could do anything without his say so. Everybody was afraid of him, including most of the adults in charge. He was pure evil. '

'But you tried to stand up to him Jack, I thought you were the bravest person I ever met.' Memories of that hateful time made Kyle shudder. 'Tell him about that thing with the kitten.'

'I'm sure Pete can imagine the cruelty an idiot like that was capable of. Except he's not an idiot, he's quite bright.'

'He's a vicious bully. He can make anybody do anything. I thought we were free of him when we moved here and I felt kind of safe with Archer around.'

'Yeah, but then we ran into him in town. He'd already got Mandy and Kellie back in his power and they needed more people to pull off this big heist.'

'I really wish we'd stayed with you at the cinema. I wanted to, I quite like James Bond, but Jack …'

'No point crying over spilt milk, what's done is done. But we can't let Archer go down because of that ars...'

'There's only one thing you can do, give yourselves up. You'd get lighter sentences.'

'Yeah but if we did that and told the police about him, he'd make our lives a misery in the young offenders place. He'd rule the roost there on the first day.'

'So maybe you need some way of trapping him so you all get caught. When they see he's running it all, you won't be in so much trouble.'

'That's easy for you to say. You've never been to these places, they're a nightmare.'

'You mean you've been there before? I thought this was your first offence.'

'It is. I only know from the other boys at the home, the stories they tell of beatings and strip searches...'

'The wardens beat you?'

'No, the other kids. And worse.'

'I can't go there Pete, I'm not strong enough to take that.' Kyle was almost in tears at the thought of it.

'There must be something we can do. Surely if they knew about all the hard work at school…'

'Yeah but Bar-stard tore up the blue slips. He's the root of all this, we should burn down the school or something.'

Peter was horrified at this suggestion. 'That would only make things worse, you'd definitely go to prison then. Look, I've had an idea, leave it with me.'

'You are joking, right. You want me to help get them off after the way they acted?' Archer had reached his limit.

'But Stiff was manipulating them, they are all terrified of him and what he'll do if they cross him.'

'I'm supposed to forgive Jack and Kyle for holding me down while he – what did he say? Smashed my face in?'

'You forgave them before, and me – I must have hurt you far more than he did. He didn't even slap you.'

'Well maybe I'm all out of mercy. I can't keep turning the other cheek to people who are kissing me one minute and calling me a turd the next.'

'Oh right. Jack told me Mandy called you that.'

'I had no idea what it was so I asked Rory. She was basically calling me a little shit.'

'But that was just for Stiff. Jack said she stood in front of him when he was taking a swing at you. That took a lot of guts, he would have hit her you know.'

'Really? He would hit a girl? That's appalling.' Stiff seemed to have power over weaker kids, similar to the way Edlyn had. But no matter how bad Edlyn was, he would never hurt a girl, it was the ultimate sin.

'Jack said he was really sorry he held your arm, but he would have let go if Stiff had started punching you. He said Mandy's courage made him ashamed and she told him that he was a coward for not standing up for you.' Peter sighed. 'I know it sounds like I'm trying to make excuses for their bad behaviour, but only because I believe they should have a second chance.'

'Because I haven't already given them a second chance.' Archer's smile reflected the grim irony.

'A third chance. That's who you are Archer, someone who inspires us to think we could be good too. If only someone would believe in us, someone like you.'

He shook his head, it was a big weight to carry on top of everything else that had gone on, but maybe this was one of the trials Kalen had forseen. The boy before him had changed for the better. He was right, it was too big a part of Archer's nature to see the good in people for him to turn his back now. 'Alright, I give in, but it must be within the law. What can I do?'

Peter hesitated, part of the plan was firmly outside the law, but maybe Archer would see the sense in it.

'No way Pete. I can't do that. I'm not even listening any more. You'll have to find another plan.'

'Come on Kyle, no-one else could do it. Jack can't, obviously, nor Archer. He doesn't know me.'

'But when he gets caught, he's going to know he was set up and then he'll come gunning for me. I'll be dead.'

'Oh for God's sake Kyle, show a bit of spine.'

'Why don't you do it then Mandy? You don't seem to be afraid of him.'

'Because I'm supposed to persuade him it's a good idea. I can't suggest it as well, it's too obvious.'

Archer was concerned that Peter's idea was too risky and had too many potential pitfalls, but he'd agreed to discuss it at what Kyle had proudly called a war council.

Jack was determined to introduce an attack on the school and more specifically the head's office into the mix. 'I'm sure there is some evidence in Barston's office that will prove he's got some kind of vendetta against us. If we can get hold of it, it would get Archer off the hook and your Mum and Dad won't lose their licence Pete.'

'What kind of evidence are you thinking of Jack?' Archer had the start of an idea.

'I don't know, something in our files, a report or that list he made the teachers sign for the blue slips.'

'They must keep records of blue slips because someone wins a prize every half term for getting the most.'

'Did you say that Stiff used to go to that school too?'

'Yeah, until he got expelled for threatening a teacher.'

'If he found out someone was breaking into the head's office, he would want to go along and do some damage.'

'What are you thinking?'

'He said that he was going to deal with me later. That means beat me up. What if he found out I was going to break in to get this report? Wouldn't he want to hurt me and wreck the room at the same time?'

'Yeah, but that's much too risky. What if he did beat you up or you were caught by the caretaker?'

'That would never happen. Not if we did it properly.'

Thirty Three

The bait was carefully laid. Kyle and Kellie "happened" to meet in town in a café where several of Stiff's informants were known to gather. They discussed either side of a conversation they had overheard between Archer and Peter. It seemed Archer was plotting to search the head's office for a special file at the weekend.

An hour later, Jack's football game on the park was interrupted by a summons from Stiff. Mandy was "invited" as she walked to a friend's house. He asked lots of questions and Jack suffered a couple of slaps rather than admit he knew anything.

'Look, I'm not asking you to do anything to him, I know you think he's a mate.'

'You can hit me all you like. He's up on a charge for your crimes and he stood by us, never said a word about any of it. I can't believe I stood there and held him while you were gonna mash him. So do your worst, you won't get anything out of me.'

'Jack, I appreciate your loyalty, I always did. Which is why I don't wanna hurt you. I've know that you want out and I'm prepared to do a deal.'

Jack pretended to consider it. 'What sort of deal?'

'Your freedom in return for information.'

'Such as?'

'What's in this file he needs so badly?'

'Information.'

'Don't prat me around. What sort of information?'

He hesitated and Mandy jumped in with, 'For God's sake, what harm could it do? Just tell him. Or I will.'

'You weren't thinking of trying to buy your way out were you Mand? You know the price of your freedom.'

'No I just want to get round to Nina's, she'll be wondering where I am. Look it's about the court cases.'

'What court cases?'

'Archer's and the foster home Jack's at.'

'Why Jack, have you been a naughty boy?'

'No, I've been trying to go straight, but Bar-stard's trying to make it look bad for us. Pete overheard a teacher talking about a report in our file.'

'And this file's got stuff that would get Saint Archer off the hook. It would be such a pity if it accidentally got destroyed in, let's say a fire or something, wouldn't it?'

'You wouldn't.'

'Wouldn't I? That'd teach you not to try and mess with me, wouldn't it?'

Jack flashed an angry look at Mandy who shrugged and looked bored as Stiff reached his decision.

'Look, I'm prepared to give you one more chance. If you can find out when this is gonna happen, I might just manage to rescue your bits of the report.'

Jack turned to go and Mandy followed, but he caught her arm. 'Where do you think you're going?'

'I told you. Round to Nina's.'

He pulled her to him and kissed her, then let her go. 'You might as well go, it's not the same when you're all dolled up like a Disney princess. When are you going to go back to your sexy style?'

'I told you, I've got to dress like this until the heat is off, the other gear was too distinctive.'

'Maybe I'll get you something decent you can change into just for me.'

She shuddered as she walked out with Jack and he held back his anger until they were round the corner. 'Why do you let him treat you like that?'

'He threatened to hurt Kellie if I don't do what he wants. I take back what I said, you're not a coward.'

He smiled at her and she grinned back, if the plan worked it would be a new life for both of them.

Obviously, they didn't tell any of the adults about their scheme, Penny and Julie would have worried and Todd and Dave would have banned it and probably grounded them for the weekend. It was harder keeping it secret from Tom and Rory, so Mandy and Archer pretended to be going out so they could discuss things in private. But she ended up telling stories about when she and Kellie were in the children's home with Jack. She wanted to hear Archer's opinion of him because Kyle had mentioned how evil he'd been and she wanted all the details.

'Come on Archer, he did more than call you names and tease you about the way you talk, that's not evil.'

'It was just the sort of stuff boys do to each other. I've had worse.'

'So he didn't threaten to shoot you with your own bow then? That's what Kyle said.'

'No. He was going to shoot an apple off my head. He would have shot me, he hadn't got a clue how to aim.'

'Oh my God. What happened? Did you beat him up?'

'No, why would you think that? Pete talked him out of it then I showed them how to use a bow properly.'

'So was he worse than the others? He was pretty mean when I knew him, but that was just to impress Stiff.'

'Like Pete was only nasty to impress Jack. But Pete came through and stood up to him when it mattered.'

'So Jack was worse then.'

'Not really, Pete had to go a step further every time.'

'Jack stood up to him like we planned, even when Stiff was slapping him around and threatening worse.'

Finally, the message got through to Archer. 'You fancy him don't you?'

'Stiff? No way. He fancies me and I have to suffer …'

'No, I meant Jack. Why do you have to suffer?'

She looked at him for a while as though trying to decide if she could trust him. Shaking her head, she sighed. 'He threatened to hurt Kellie if I didn't do what he said. He would too, I've seen the way he looks at her.'

'Swine. I can't stand boys that even threaten to hurt girls, he needs to be taught a lesson. One that he won't forget in a hurry.'

It had been fairly straightforward to plant the final piece of information, that Archer was going to do the deed at five o'clock on Saturday.

'And you're sure he'll be on his own?'

'Yeah. He hasn't got any friends apart from Peter and he'll be away visiting relatives.' Jack played his part well, just the right amount of reluctance.

'Excellent. This couldn't be better. Well Jack, if it all works out, I might consider letting you go. You're boring me now with all this going straight shit. You've lost the fire in your belly. I need to have people I can trust.'

So the scene was set. Jack came away with some relief, it was the first time in almost a year he would not be dancing to someone else's tune. Somehow he had to believe that he was worth more than the nasty piece of work he had become.

There was one big flaw with their scheme, but it couldn't be helped. They overlooked the fact that Stiff was such a coward that he would never tackle Archer on his own so he insisted on forcing Darren and a couple of others along for the job. The security fence was no challenge at all to fit young men and they moved like shadows in the dark. The school was an eerie place on a damp, chilly Saturday evening, their footsteps echoed as they crossed the playground.

'Right, one of you stay here and keep an eye out for the caretaker. He's probably sat watching telly, but if you see anything, throw a stone up to Bar-stard's office. That's the big window up on the first floor. As he pointed, they saw a flicker of light and ducked behind the hedge. 'Look's like he's up there, just like Jack said.'

'What are you gonna do if he fights?'

'What do you think? After the way he's buggered up the whole shoplifting scam, I'm gonna beat the crap out of him. If you're pussy, you can wait in the hallway in case bug-a-lugs here lets the caretaker past.'

'He might come from another direction.'

'So watch them all. Right, everyone set? Come on then.'

At the back of the building, Stiff climbed up to the window in the boys' toilets and forced the broken catch easily. They climbed in, creeping through the dark, empty corridors. As they approached the door to the head's office a siren sounded somewhere in the distance and they were frozen to the spot.

'It's alright, it's probably just an ambulance or something. If anyone comes, just bang on the door then get the hell out. Come on then Darren.'

They opened the door to the outer office and crept in, watching the beam of torchlight moving as though someone was looking for something. They sneaked in expecting to surprise Archer, but got the worst shock of their lives. Both boys were blinded as black hoods were thrown over their heads, their arms were bent backwards and their wrists shackled tightly. Stiff heard a shout of protest, a thump, then sounds of a struggle.

'Get him out of here, stick him with the others, we'll deal with them later.'

'What's going on? Who are you?'

'Shut up. You speak only when you are spoken to.'

Thirty Four

For the first time in his life, Stiff was in the same position as his victims, helpless and afraid with someone else calling the shots. But unlike his victims, he was not an innocent being forced to take part in some kind of criminal activity. He listened as the frighteningly cold voice described some of the terrifying things that would happen to him if he did not do as he was told. He was sitting in a chair in the headmaster's study, with his own belt securing his wrists to the chair's back. His ankles were bound to the legs of the chair and every time he did not do as he was told there was a pinprick on his arm.

The voice was relentless, it told him that he had one chance now to put things right, to atone for all his sins and save the souls of those that he had tried to destroy. The scariest part was that he had no idea how many people were in the room, where they were or what they would do next. He had no personal courage at the best of times and this was definitely not one of those. At last, the voice gave its final instruction, he must confess to everything, the way he had organised the gang and bullied the children involved and terrorised them with threats and violence until they were forced to do his bidding.

A final pinprick on his arm was enough to convince him to tell all, he heard the click of a tape recorder and knew that his words were being recorded, but his fear of the consequences was so strong now that he told it all, leaving nothing out. This little scam was just the latest in a long line of similar schemes lasting several years. At every place he stayed he had stolen, bullied and hurt people. Initially, this was to get material things, then because he enjoyed the power and at the end, just because he could.

Once he started talking, it was as though he couldn't stop, every last little detail about his sad, shady life came out. He was so desperate to name all of his victims and all of the atrocities he had committed, that he didn't hear his interrogator silently leave the room and escape. Stiff was still talking as the young man entered the room, his gun pointed warily at each of the corners of the room before bringing it to rest at the babbling figure. Normally the detective would have announced his arrival, but a notice taped to the door read "CAUTION! Taped confession in progress."

Forensic science was unable to determine much evidence from the note apart from the facts that it was printed on standard photocopy quality paper from an inkjet printer; the font type was Arial black and the font size was 72pt. Thin rubber gloves had been used to handle the paper and the tape was Sellotape, cut with scissors. Some kind of synthesiser had been used to disguise the voice that gave the information on the 999 call. The best they could manage was that three or four different voices had read the short message simultaneously. The music playing fairly loudly in the background was the Guns N' Roses version of "Live and Let Die".

Although the confession was extracted under duress, they were able to question the suspect directly about the crimes and having admitted to them already, it didn't make sense for him to try and deny anything. It was a good collar; several unsolved crimes were cleared as a result of it. Three other suspects were caught on the school premises, questioned and charged. This may have had some bearing on the detective's willingness for leniency when it came to some of the other individuals implicated in the confessions. At Archer's suggestion, his four friends had written statements outlining their part in the two stealing sprees and these had been handed into the police station that same night along with some of the stolen goods still in a saleable state.

The first thing Penny and Todd knew about any of it was when the young detective came round to the house with a woman he introduced as D.C. Bell.

'Oh dear, I hope this doesn't mean more trouble.' Penny looked over at Archer with a worried expression.

'Yes and no. I'm pleased to report that Don has been completely cleared of all charges against him. We now know that he had nothing to do with any of the thefts and he was only attempting to return the stolen goods.'

'I never doubted it for an instant.'

'However,' the detective fixed Archer with a hard stare, 'we would appreciate if you wouldn't take things into your own hands young man. If you are aware of a crime being committed, it is your civic duty to inform the police, not wage some kind of vigilante action to undo the crime.'

Archer looked down at the floor. Something about the man's quietly purposeful manner made him respond with the due respect, but nothing would ever prevent him from trying to do what he could to reverse injustice and he didn't want the man to read that in his eyes. 'Yes sir.'

Pausing for a second before allowing a few degrees of warmth to heat his voice, the detective continued. 'I am sure you were acting for the benefit of your friends and this is one of the contributory factors in the CPS's decision not to prosecute four of the perpetrators.' He looked over to where Mandy and Kellie were sitting on the sofa, nervously gripping each other's hands. 'Apparently you have had such a good influence on them that several of their teachers are prepared to stand up and testify as character witnesses.'

As the implications of his words pierced their anxiety, revealing the tentative smiles underneath, he addressed them directly. 'Amanda and Kellie Brogan, you will both be required to register at the station for a period of one year's probation. You will also need to continue with your reformed behaviour and stay out of trouble for the whole year or you will go straight to a youth offenders' institute. You must both attend a number of compulsory sessions to help with your rehabilitation. The stores have kindly agreed they will drop all charges if you complete the required community service programme.'

'Yes sir.'

The ghost of a smile twitched the corner of his lips at their lively display of relief and gratitude, involving lots of hugs and high fives, then Mandy spoke. 'Please sir, could you tell me anything about the two boys, Jack and Kyle? Will they be under probation as well?'

'I'm afraid I cannot discuss another case, but I'm sure they will be contacting you shortly after my visit.'

'What about the headmaster's attempt to get Julie's licence revoked? There must be something we can do to help her, it's completely unjustified.' Penny was upset at the thought of her friend's troubles.

'That is not a police matter, it is in the hands of social services, but in view of the irregularities in the case, we will be passing on any information we uncover during our investigation. I can't say any more on the matter.'

Archer couldn't be sure, but there was just the brief twitch of an eyelid that looked suspiciously like a wink, then they got up, turning at the door. 'I don't suppose there's any point in asking where you were on Saturday night between five and six or if anyone saw you?'

Archer's face reflected total innocence as he said, 'We were all together in the town, but I don't suppose anyone else would remember seeing us and we didn't speak to anybody.'

'Just as I thought.'

Penny saw them out to the car and was embarrassed by the racket coming from the house as her charges celebrated with plenty of noise. D.C. Bell smiled warmly. 'You have raised some lovely children, Mrs Gardner.'

'I know. That's why I'm so annoyed that people like that headmaster and shop owner can get away with trying to hurt them by lying and ...'

'There is absolutely no chance of that, I assure you. Justice will be done.'

Epilogue

'So let me get this straight, you outwitted this evil gang leader, got him and his minions put in jail, and set free the poor children he had under his spell.' Finn was impressed.

'I guess you might say that.'

'And in the process, three of the boys and two girls were released from the wicked enchantment that turned them into rogues and ruffians.' Fletch added his bit.

Archer was beginning to wonder rather uneasily where this was heading. 'Something like that.'

'And one of these girls had set her sights on you, trying to enchant you into courting her.'

'Well yes, but …'

'Stop being so modest Archer, we can tell that you only gave us half the details. I'm sure if we were to pass this onto Doug he'd soon turn it into a song that would make the tale worthy of the telling.'

'And he's prepared to give us a handsome payment for such a tale. Apparently "Archer son of Sedge" was worth every cent he paid for it, a thousand times over.'

'What? You mean someone sold him my story? Was it you Fletch? Or you Finn?' He grabbed the front of their tunics as he challenged them.

They were laughing at his pretend anger and Fletch finally admitted who it was.

Archer laughed. 'Well in that case, I don't begrudge a single coin. If Hereward managed to feed his band for a week, then good luck to him. Despite everything we've been told about the renegades, he was a man of honour.'

Acknowledgements

Thank you to everyone who has helped me to believe in myself – without you, Archer would never have lived outside of my imagination and my computer's hard drive.

Special thanks to the following – you know the part you played and mere words cannot express my gratitude: Jo, Debby, Norman, Lynne, Steph, Sam, Rachel, Brian, Char, Kevin, Kerry, Karl, Hannah, Sarah, Anthony and Holly.

Thank you to all those people I have plagued for their opinions on the ideas, words, artwork and everything else needed to bring this massive undertaking to fruition.

A big thank you to Kevin Hicks at History Squad, Kerry at Angel Path Inspiration, Karl at Knights of Middle England, Brian at Chalice Well, Andy & Ella Portman at Livingtao and Rachel at Millbatch Farm for their technical expertise – any remaining mistakes are of my own making.

The next adventure in this series is Reagan. If you would like a taster, read on:

This couldn't be happening. Not again. Reagan threw down his precious notebook and pencil in disgust. He had tried a hundred different ways to solve this puzzle and nothing worked. It was no longer just an interesting challenge. If he didn't solve this thing soon, more people in the village were going to suffer the consequences of the dreadful run of bad luck and accidents. The devastation was just getting worse.

Closing his eyes against the pain in his head, he ground the heels of his hands into his eyelids as though it would help, or at least drive the demons out of his head. That just created white lights which remained even after he opened his eyes. He was angry with himself for imagining his gift was so special that he could solve the problem many of the best minds in the village had been working on for over a decade. It must be him. He had all the same symptoms as the other boys, a lot stronger than they had from what Malduc suggested.

Cradling his chin in his hands, he closed his eyes once more. The bright lights were still there, but like everything else around him, they were trying to tell him something. He relaxed and let his mind run freely as the crazy shapes tumbled around, using the back of his eyelids as their playground. He held his breath as two or three thoughts detached themselves from the jumble and vied with each other to seek his attention. One of them broke away, heading to the part of his brain that turned the germ of an idea into a recognisable thought in a language he could understand. Just as it was about to make it, his pencil decided to roll off the table and fall on the floor. It was a small sound, but more than enough to destroy his concentration before the thought reached the forefront of his brain where it could stand up and be counted.

He could have cried out in anger, but that would have given him no physical release, so he shoved everything off the table with violent satisfaction as books and papers tumbled down, landing with a pleasing crash. But not quite pleasing enough. He dropped his head so that his forehead connected with the work-worn wood with a thump that came close to causing actual pain.

Suddenly, it was as though everything his father said about not learning anything without suffering first came true. All three thoughts presented themselves to the correct part of his brain with their hair neatly combed and their bags packed, ready to go.

The first thought was that it was not one big shape but several. The shapes spinning round in front of his eyes were triangles, squares and pentagons, but that was just to give him a clue.

The second thought was that the patterns written in the crops would help him to find the number he needed. He knew it was all about the sequences, and this would tell him which pattern to focus on.

The third thought was that he needed to talk to Archer. His hero was probably the only person who could help him solve the mystery before it destroyed him.